THREE OF ME

DIYA GWALANI

ISBN

Hardcase 979-8-89588-662-5
Paperback 979-8-89498-841-2

Somewhere in the pages of history

The world will know a love so strong

Lived to defy right and wrong

Sang the words to an empty song.

Somewhere in the pages of history

Etched in eternity

The world will know a love so strong

But she will never know

And he will never know.

I extend a deep sense of gratitude for the Grace that chose me to write this book.

Contents

Part Three

Prologue

Rocking to and fro, ever so slowly in my brown teakwood chair, I stare out at the snowfall on my window. I wonder how much of my hair matches the colour of the snow! The long French windows of my home shield me from the bitter cold outside, as I sit sipping my tea and reflecting on the years behind me.

Time. What a strange word. A paradox in itself. An anticipatory minute that never ends, and a 'blink-of-an-eye' lifetime. Like different planes of existence, fragments of consciousness – each joining the other through dimensions of organic symmetry and divine geometry.

I look back completely mesmerised – like a hypnotic awareness had led me to the path that I was meant to take… a strange sense of calm filling me. I laugh at the irony of it all. How I wish I had the calm when I needed it the most! All those years of struggle, all those moments that I felt like giving up. I admired the courage of nature. To stand tall in the face of a storm and shed its garb when it needs to, to renew its senses when the time comes, and to adapt to cruelty as beautifully as adapting to compassion, trusting the creator. Why wasn't I able to do that all those years? Always conflicting, never trusting?

My wisdom tells me had I not been at the bottom, how would I climb my way up to the top? Surely no one is born afloat in the skies of tenderness. Each of us has our own staircase to climb, and at necessary intervals, they spiral with the staircases of necessary people. What an experience it has been. *Old age brings with it a wisdom that the youth can only be grateful to partake of.* Although it brings with it a senile hope to turn back time.

What I comprehend as the essence of life is to stand by your beliefs, to believe in your convictions, to be convinced of your choices, and to choose what your heart says. To realise that the difficult times are not the ones to bail on. They are rather the tests in your life, checking if you're growing into the strong individual that you are meant to be. They are the testing waters of your relationships, assuring you that they are getting stronger with the endurance of hardships.

I'm finally at peace and at ease with myself. After years of looking for love, I feel it now for my own soul and my own journey. Albeit it has taken me my whole life and each experience woven together to understand that the external circumstances are only a mirror of the inner struggle. The perspective of what is happening within us connects the dots with the happenings around us, and unites them with the same essence. There is an intrinsic connection between the happenings *inside us and around us.* Like a branch which needs to exist on a tree, a tree needs the branches to exist. Today, I feel complete – standing at the beginning of the end. I'm standing where the grass is green, in the centre of the storm – in the nexus. I stand unwavering in the realm of reality... everything resonating in complete synchronicity and the symphony of life echoing with the truth of nothing.

Preface

Deep inside the woods, I hear the sound of strings,
Of a hundred years of a mystic past, the resonance
still stings.

'What are you reading Saru?' Alisha asked her daughter Sara, as she was flipping through the pages of an old tattered handmade notebook, its pages bound by a string and feathers stuck on the cover.

'It's some poetry I found in your loft, ma.' She replied.

'Whose is it, ma?' asked Nikhil. He bent down to pick up a photo album that had fallen.

'Ma, these are like a treasure from your past! Is that you on the blue bench with uncle?'

Alisha stirred from within. She slowly walked up to where the kids were standing, emptying the lofts, books, and belongings from years ago, all scattered. Specks of dust shone in the cold, bright rays sneaking in from the windows. She nervously extended her hand and flipped the pages, a teary smile escaping her quivering lips.

There were collections of Dev's poetry, quotes and doodles and so many photo albums. They were a precious possession of her past and an anchor of her childhood and teenage years. Sara came closer to her mum, and they read together.

'Is this the collection of Dev uncle, you had mentioned to show me once?'

'Yes.' she nodded. They read on…

Deep inside the woods, I hear the sound of strings, of a hundred years of a mystic past, the resonance still stings.

Trapped in an antique treasury, filled with mistakes and dust, I take out my guitar, now completely rust.

Goosebumps spread over her wrinkled skin as she thought longingly about the days gone by.

PART ONE

Chapter 1

The air brimmed with magic, the slight drizzle adding to the dreamy atmosphere. Everyone rose to attention for the flag hoisting, and Mrs. Devon, in her crisp, lemon-coloured sari went up to the piano and microphone on the dais. Her beautiful voice sent goose bumps to everyone present. The intensity with which she sang the National Anthem filled the air with vibrancy, inspiration, and positivity. Alisha imagined herself in the same way, singing the anthem one day in front of such a big crowd. She was very passionate about singing. From when she was little, singing was as much a part of her as talking! Since she always showed such an unwavering interest in her hobby, her parents had enrolled her in one of the finest vocal training academies in the city.

The Republic Day parade was one of the most exciting and lively ones that took place in Shimla. The State-level Republic Day parade was held every year on 26th January at the Ridge Maidan, which was the hub of all cultural activities in the city. Running east to west alongside the famous Mall Road, the Ridge was a massive open space right in the centre of Shimla. It was the heart of the city, quite literally, hosting all the city's most prominent celebrations, festivals and government affairs. The immensely beautiful structure of Christ Church was its main attraction. Lit up in the snowy evenings, it filled the arena with the grace of a mighty king, holding his kingdom in loving entirety.

This year, most of the schools in the city had their students attending and participating in the parade.

'Inculcating the spirit of patriotism in the youth instils in them a sense of belonging and unparalleled respect'; with that she ended her closing address.

Alisha stood in the middle of the crowd, taking it all in. Alisha – standing to attention with her neatly braided hair in her white shirt and blue pleated skirt – was mesmerised. At 16, she was not your conventional teenager. Emotional and bright, she was the perfect balance of vivaciousness and maturity. She watched in awe as the high school students of her Alma Mater – Bishop Cotton's – took part in the parade. She felt sentimental. It was the first time she had experienced a connection with the glory of her country. As she watched the marching soldiers in their uniforms and our tricoloured beauty adorning the proud skies, feelings of respect and admiration brewed in her big heart and tiny mind.

All the dignitaries stood with their heads held high. Aarav, the head boy of the school, gave the honouring speech to the chief guest of the ceremony. Aarav was Dev's older brother. Dev and Alisha had been best friends since they met.

He and Alisha were in the same class since the first grade and were inseparable. Like two peas in a pod, they were hardly seen without each other. They would sit for hours together without realising how much time had passed. From writing poetry to imaginary games and silly squabbles to serious arguments, they had an array of experiences. Their routine every day was a mandatory visit to the blue bench in the garden of their apartment, where they would spend hours pondering, chatting, snacking, and planning their lives.

Alisha looked across to the boy's line where he was standing, right behind in the seventh row, and smiled at him, a proud younger brother. The entire school applauded the speech.

The three of them were waiting eagerly to celebrate Dev's birthday after the event. Alisha & him were born a week apart and often kick-started the celebrations with his birthday.

Chapter 2

'*Ting, Tong*' '*Ting, Tong*'

'Dev, open the door!' yelled his mum from inside the kitchen.

'On it, Mum!' He rushed to the door. Alisha and a few other friends had come over to their house for Dev's 17th birthday, and his parents had also invited the extended family and their close friends over for dinner. Aarav's friends would be joining in, too.

Dev was a thinker, and Aarav, a go-getter. While Dev was quiet and interacted with just his close friends in a small circle, Aarav was Mr. Popular, young, dynamic, and dashing. Aarav had it all: the charm, the intelligence, and a kind heart. He was a protective older brother to Dev, 3 years senior, and he was academically and culturally a star in school.

Everyone knew him, and to know him was to love him. The brothers bore a striking resemblance physically, though, taking after their mum's side of the family. Their father was a government employee in the city, working for the Income Tax department. A family of 4, they resided in Clifton Valley Apartments on Junga Road.

'*Happy Birthday to you! Happy Birthday to you!*'

Dev cringed. He detested the extra attention on him, although he loved having everyone over! He saw Alisha smirking as she knew how he felt socially awkward. Everyone exchanged pleasantries and sat down to play games, eat dinner, and listen to music. It was after an hour that Aarav came out of his room, all eyes on him.

'Happy Birthday, bro!' He playfully punched Dev and greeted the other guests. The snowy drizzle made the evening delightful as everyone were engrossed in good conversation, good company, and great food.

The brink of adolescence is where childhood meets adulthood.

It was almost 9:30 pm, and Alisha had to be home before 10. Although she lived in the next block of Clifton apartments, her parents had set strict curfews for her. As she said bye to everyone, Aarav offered to walk her down. In the cool and crisp air, they chatted about how wonderful the day was: the lovely parade, his speech, the vibe of the event, and ending the day with Dev's birthday dinner!

'By the way, you look lovely, Alisha! Yellow really suits you...'

Alisha blushed. He leaned in to give her a good night hug, something that he had never done before. Alisha felt a strange mix of excitement, nervousness, and exhaustion.

'Thanks, Aarav! Good night.'

Alisha went home and spent some time with her parents. It had been a long day, but thankfully, the next day was a holiday. They sat together, and as her dad watched the re-run of the news, her mother was reading on the sofa. She sprawled on her mother's lap and fell asleep. An hour later, she shifted to her room. Thoughts of Aarav filled her mind, but she didn't know what to make of it. She thought she would discuss it with Dev the next day… after all, what are best friends for? Since they had been best friends since the first grade, the understanding that they shared was beyond their years. They also had a good group among a few of them, classmates who also lived in the same colony. Their parents were pretty comfortable if they made plans to go out, as they knew each other well.

Alisha waited at the blue bench in the huge garden between their apartments, the place Dev and she usually met before their school walk. They would sometimes stroll along the hillside and have hot chai before the day began. He came in a bit late and asked to borrow some notes. As Alisha mindlessly searched in her bag, he noticed she was preoccupied.

'What's up?'

'Dude! Last evening, when we were winding up, Aarav walked me down. You were speaking to Harsh and Anna at that point, I think. When we said bye, he leaned in to hug me! It was super weird. Then he complimented me, saying I look really good and yellow really suits me and all…so weird, right?'

'Whaaat?' His face scrunched up. 'Really? My brother? Hahaha!'

'What's funny?'

'Nothing, it just doesn't sound like him with you. I've hardly seen you 2 interact. I mean, it's just funny in my head, sorry. Why are you reading so much into it, though? Do you feel something is on his mind?'

'No, not like that... it just never happened before, and it felt strange, so I thought I'd speak to you about it... clearly, it isn't a good idea!'

'Haha! I didn't even say anything! You're overreacting.'

Alisha felt a tug in her stomach and turned away. She looked into her bag again before he could tease her. They walked in silence for a few minutes. As they neared school, they exchanged notes and other information. They decided to meet in the evening for a game of tennis at the recreation centre of her apartment after she had finished her vocal training class.

Chapter 3

Take all this pain and make it into something beautiful,
don't let it go in vain.

'A little lower, Alisha, the pitch is too high.'

Mr. Anthony was patient but stern. His white hair and beard made him look like a wizard, and when his fingers touched the piano, the magic was evident.

Alisha trained for singing at the *Strong Song* Music Academy thrice a week. She loved to sing, and she had been training there since she was 9. It was harder than she thought, especially on days when she had probably eaten a bit too much or hadn't slept well, it impacted the quality of her voice. When she was about 14 years old, Sir Anthony had put her on certain breathing exercises as well to help her round her tone, make her voice fuller, and extend her vocal range.

She was currently training to sing in the *Voice of Himachal* Singing Competition. It was a state-wide competition held every year and had 3 age categories. She had chosen to perform an acoustic rendition of the song 'I Will Survive' by Gloria Gaynor. What a fantastic but difficult choice it was, she realised after she began practising for it! Sir would not let her back out now, and the range was too up and down, too erratic for her. She felt herself lacking confidence and slipping into a mental lethargy. This was getting very difficult.

'I need a break, Sir.'

'Ten minutes. The preliminary rounds begin next week, and we need to finish the last 60 seconds.'

She went to the water cooler and sat down. She felt her body tremble with a strange sense of fear. It happened a lot of late, and she didn't know what to do about it. When she told Dev and her mum, they both said she worried easily... but this felt different. This was not worrying. Like suddenly her heart would race, her breath would quicken, and she would be zoned out for a few minutes, breaking into a sweat too.

She felt preoccupied on most days. She was physically present but mentally all over the place. She said a silent prayer and went back into the recording aisle. With a deep breath, she started to sing. She completely changed the pace of the song. She was very nervous, thinking Sir Anthony would angrily stop her, but with a fist of courage, she began her very own version of the song... slow and melodious, nothing like the original fast-paced track.

A minute had passed, and he just stared at her. As she finished the 90 second baritone, she looked at him with anticipation. He extended his hand to her.

'You finally found your style and your voice, Alisha! That was incredible.'

'Thank you, Sir!' she burst into tears...

'What happened?' He was worried. Was he too harsh on her earlier? He thought to himself.

'Is everything alright?'

'Yes, Sir, I'm sorry. I just need a moment.'

She excused herself, and the next couple of students walked in to perform their duo trial. She went back to the water cooler and composed herself. She took her bag and started to walk towards the back exit when she saw Aarav with his friends right at the entrance of Cove Café, just across the street. He noticed her too, and saw her picking up her backpack to leave. He crossed to the other side and entered the studio.

'How come you're leaving earlier than usual today?' he asked.

'Just one of those days. I couldn't get my head around it today! I'll go inform sir and bounce...'

'Come, join us for lunch.'

'Nah, I'll go home. I'm a bit out of sorts.'

'Just for half an hour, let's share a pizza...' He stepped in closer and held her hand.

She felt wobbly, like a mild electric current passing through her stomach and legs. Her heart raced quicker, and her face was flushed.

'Ok, let me just tell you, and Sir...I actually need to get my stuff also,' she was kind of stammering. She came out in a few minutes.

They walked into the café. She knew all his friends. Rohit, Sasha, Ajay, and Ritika had been friends since second grade. There was a time when they would all get into silly fights with Alisha and Dev's friends. Being 3 years younger than their batch, they were always at the receiving end of their banter. But as time passed, a certain maturity set in, and now they all hung out together. As they sipped on cold coffee and waited for the pizza, Aarav leaned in closer to her.

'Why does your beautiful face look so worried?'

'Aru! I have to ask you directly – what is with this weird way of talking to me of late?'

'Weird? Like that's what you call it?'

'Don't be silly! No offence. It's just different, you've never spoken to me like that. Your gestures have been overwhelming, okay, flirtatious. And I just wanted to ask you directly instead of beating around the bush...'

He didn't know what to say. Alisha had always been someone who would say what was on her mind without even thinking, while he probably didn't expect a direct conversation. At that age, boys were playful, or maybe even as they grew older, her mum would say. But Aarav didn't know what to say... They ate in silence, and they headed for home. He would often hang out with many girls, and he was used to them giving him a lot of attention. But he could not get in that zone with Alisha, she had a way of making people be completely themselves in her company.

Alisha ambushed her mind for being so direct. She was restless. She went home and to her room, took out her tennis outfit, racket, and shoes, and lay down, tossing and turning. She put on some music to calm down before heading to the recreation centre.

Chapter 4

'What a game!' Whose anger are you directing at me?'

He was always cracking silly jokes, and she rolled her eyes.

'Alright, alright! What's going on? You seem heated up.'

'Nothing ya. I spoke to your brother and asked him directly. He didn't say anything. Just felt like I made a fool of myself.'

'What did he say? What did you ask him exactly?'

'Well, I asked him why he was being weird with me… now that I'm saying it out loud to you… maybe he didn't take it the right way…'

'Hmm… Maybe. He usually is weird with girls his own age!' he smirked.

'It's just that I have a lot going on apart from all of this. My vocal training isn't up to the mark, I'm not landing a good range. And the competition is just 2 months away! Math is driving me crazy, and ever since these encounters with Aarav, I find myself distracted. It feels like something is different.'

Dev walked a few steps and sat on the chair outside the court. He looked pensive and was quiet while she felt strange.

'Say something.'

'You like him?'

'I think I've started to think about him. I don't know what it is yet, but I don't dislike him.'

'From where I see it, you need to be more emotionally contained, for now at least.'

'Meaning?'

'Meaning... like be the cup that holds your coffee. Don't overspill. I feel like you get so emotionally overwhelmed lately. I'm not saying it's a good or bad thing. I'm just saying figure out what works for you. You are probably being too harsh on your vocal training; you need to breathe before you attempt Math, and with Aru, you are probably beginning to like him. I don't know, I'm guessing, too, but it's your first time, so don't get too swayed away by all your thoughts. Things will figure themselves out.'

'My God Dev! Are you smoking something? Did all this insight actually come from you?'

'Just because I'm humorous doesn't mean I'm dumb, right?'

'It's not that. We've known each other forever, and you have never given me such a speech. I was wondering where it's coming from. Tell me more about this emotional containment.'

'That's because you don't listen to half the things I try to tell you. For a change, you are listening instead of arguing, haha!'

'Come, let's go to the blue bench, and then you tell me more... the weather is good for a stroll, let's go...' she gave him her hand to get moving.

'There's nothing more to tell you... It's like how a wave is always going to be part of the ocean. Similarly, your thoughts and emotions will always be a part of you. Sometimes, you will feel engulfed, and sometimes you may feel you are floating atop. Containment is all about feeling like you're holding something in a vessel, and holding on will ensure you feel grounded through your emotions. I don't know if it makes sense to you, it is something I have been journaling about.'

He was an avid reader, and at his age, not many people were ready to dive into deep thinking.

Alisha smiled and leaned in to give him a hug. They sat for a long time and chatted before saying goodbye. It was a long day, and she wanted to sleep early. As she walked back home, she felt a bit at peace, hoping she wouldn't lose that feeling. She loved how she felt in his company. He understood her every emotion. Everything she wanted to say, he would probably already know. It was her free space to express herself, and she was beginning to realise that without it, she didn't know who she was. It was something she had grown up with and, hence, completely reliant on.

Dev walked up the stairs to his home. He opened his journal to write, but the pen didn't move on paper. He stared blankly at the previous pages he had written. In anger, he ripped a page. He felt something break inside him, and his eyes welled up. *His first love, and she would never even know?*

What was this sudden menacing feeling that surrounded him? He tried to make sense of it, but it confused him more. In his heart, it was always him and her together, sitting by the blue bench and experiencing life. Now that she looked in a different direction, he felt a sense of threat. He was afraid of his feelings, of change.

Chapter 5

Had we known better, we would have done better.

'If it doesn't fit in the divine geometry, it will have to change its course,' Naina was explaining. Dev and she met at the restaurant near the lakeside and ordered 2 coffees. They met often, and he had a keen interest in learning more about the subtle precisions of existence. She had a lot of knowledge to offer, and he was very happy to constantly learn.

Naina was 6 years older than Dev. Their parents were friends, and Naina was always very fond of him. He was younger, but a great listener and very patient. As family friends, they had visited many holy places together and had enjoyed many fun vacations as well. On many such occasions, Naina and he would be engrossed in conversation about the spectrum of human emotions, how it's connected to the universal force, and so on. They would often be teased by their families in good humour, but they were the agony aunts of many friends and relatives!

'What does that even mean?'

'Basically, it's like this – every atom has its course – it exists in a particular way to fit amongst millions of other atoms. If you take one away, the entire configuration is different; hence, the existence of each atom is imperative to its own structure and to the structures of those around it.

It is designed by a force you cannot see. Similarly, on all levels, we are also part of a cosmic design. Our feelings tend to determine our actions. However, the universe is constantly trying to teach us perseverance,' she tried to explain.

'No, I cannot understand. It's going over my head.'

'Let it be. What is bothering you, Dev? You look unsettled today.'

'It's just stupid. But ever since Aarav and Alisha have been talking often, I've sensed undercurrents of feelings there, and that makes me feel really uncomfortable and different. Maybe insecure, like things are changing. I also feel senseless. I don't know what I want, but now I know this is making me very uneasy. I can't be myself with her. I think I'm jealous that she is sort of attracted to him.' He felt really embarrassed after hearing himself say it out loud.

'There is nothing stupid about it. I always knew you harboured feelings for her.'

'What? When have I ever said that? Don't simply say all this!'

'It's nothing that you said. It is just something I've felt, got a vibe, sort of a thing...'

She continued... 'Every relationship has its time and destiny, Dev. I know it probably feels like rock bottom, but there may be other things that would surface if you try to be a part of something that you're not meant to be a part of.

'But we've known each other since we were 6, Naina. I probably never thought of her in a romantic way, but I sure never thought of anyone else, either. In my head, it has always been me and her from one phase to another. I guess I wasn't prepared to see her eyes twinkling for someone else, let alone my own brother. Where does this leave me…and what exactly am I supposed to tell her? Things are going to change in either scenario – if I tell her I feel this way, it is directly coming in between her and him, which is not right. If I don't tell her how I feel, then I will not be able to be myself with her, and then again, she will pick up on that instantaneously… I really don't know what I am supposed to do…

'And you know what's more weird? If she hadn't had this little jingle with Aarav, I probably would have never known that I felt this way about her. Why didn't you ever tell me if you thought I had feelings for her?'

'Ha ha! It isn't my place to randomly put thoughts in your head, no! How will I just tell you? It was just something that crossed my mind a couple of times, I guess.'

They sipped their coffee in silence. This was difficult. Naina felt bad for him. At the same time, she knew it was just a doorway opening to other experiences, but not everyone looks at so many perspectives while trapped in an emotional rut. She was lost in thought for a few moments about her own struggles. She had just come out of a strange marriage.

'Look, Dev, it's like this… what you are facing right now is disappointment from a situation. It is… as if to say that the feeling you have been holding on to since a little boy, of emotional security and of warmth, has changed. All of life is an experiential journey of these feelings. You need to find something else which will make you feel secure again. It may not necessarily be a relationship, but it can be. Or it could be something else. Something that makes you feel like you have found your purpose. I know it sounds like Greek & Latin to you right now, but if you look deeper, pain is a doorway just like joy.'

Dev was as blank as an empty book.

Naina tried to pacify him, but she didn't know what he was thinking. She could sense his pain. As the famous quote by Anne Frank goes – *'for in its innermost depths, youth is lonelier than old age'.* That always resonated within her, and she could now sense it in his experience, too. The insecurities he felt were relatable to her; his restlessness was palpable.

They called for their bill and went for a walk beside the lake.

'Want to meet tomorrow morning? Say, around 6?' she asked.

'I'm not sure. I may have assignments due. I have to finish them. How about the day after?'

'I'm leaving the day after for my seminar in Delhi.'

Naina had just begun her first year of MSc. in Psychology. She had resumed her studies a few months after her marriage didn't work out, and it was quite hard on her and her family. Her 2 elder sisters were pillars of emotional strength and really helped her emotionally and to pick herself up.

She had been married for 2 years before things started to fall apart. She had married a man named Sunil through a matrimonial site. Her profile was up for fun; one she had made along with some friends whose parents were interested in looking out for them. She had found a match and agreed to meet. He was 5 years older to her, working in a software company, had a stable income, and had a pleasant demeanour.

But a few months into their marriage, things fell apart. Things he never told her earlier. He had cheated his family in property settlements, sort of a con man, and with time, she figured he was untruthful most of the time. He seemed to be attached to her, but he was never physically around, and he always gave her vague answers, even when she asked specific questions. She tried a lot to get through to him, but he kept her in a web of deceit and lies. She blamed herself for being naïve, but she couldn't put a finger on what exactly went wrong. Her family was forcing her to get out of it before things could get more complicated, and since then, she had trudged along trying to find herself again. She barely gave anyone details about the hell she went through, but she found refuge in resuming her studies.

'Oh, okay. I guess I'll make it tomorrow. You're gone for a week, right?'

'Yeah, let's try to meet tomorrow. If we have time, we can visit the monastery as well.'

'Sounds good'

They walked the long route home.

Dev was journaling in his room when Aarav walked in.

'Where have you been, dude?'

'I was out with Naina for a bit. What's up?'

'Alisha called for you like a dozen times! You were supposed to show up at her preliminary rehearsal today or something.'

'Oh my God! I completely forgot. She is going to kill me.'

Aarav felt pinched; he would have liked to be there too.

Dev stormed out of his room. Even though it was breaking his heart, he could not bear to break hers and upset her. He was supposed to meet her at the Albert Hall for her rehearsal day, and in the web of his emotions, it had completely slipped out of his mind. He didn't even know how to explain himself, she would get all over the top.

He went to her apartment on the 7th floor and rang the doorbell.

Alisha was at the dining table having soup with her parents. They welcomed Dev and offered him some, too. He sat down and exchanged pleasantries with the family. He asked Alisha if they could go for a stroll. She took her jacket, mentioned it to her parents, and went down. It was a cold evening, and she was silent until he spoke.

'I can't say sorry, it feels so fake. I feel terrible. How did it go?'

'Where were you?'

'With Naina, by the lakeside café. I don't know how it slipped out of my mind.'

Alisha was irritated and looked away.

He went and sat on the blue bench, and took a sip of his water. She took her time to come and sit near him.

'You have been incorrigible for the last few days. What is going on? You have been with me every single day of these rehearsals, and you knew how worried I was.'

She felt the familiar tremors running through her. She heard the sound of her heartbeat and was holding her head in her hands. Panic waved through her, and she struggled to find her voice. He felt she needed to seek help for these panic attacks but was afraid to tell her. Suddenly, everything was different. He would have told her things effortlessly before, but now he was so conscious of everything he said to her.

'I... I'm sorry, Alisha. I should have been there. I don't want to make up any excuse... how did it go?'

'I got selected for the finals...'

'Oh my God! Are you for real? You are so dramatic!' he laughed heartily.

'The way you look right now, you look like a wreck! I thought it would have gone horribly! Why are you sulking? To guilt trip me, eh?'

She laughed.

'I'm so, so sorry I missed it! Congratulations!' He gave her a tight hug for a few seconds before stepping back.

She smiled a relieved smile. Having him by her side was the most reassuring feeling.

'It was insane, but I was extremely nervous. After the preliminaries, we were put into groups of 10: A, B, and C. We were then told to perform some group songs on the spot. After some time, they announced 3 people per group to get through to the next round, and from the 12 of us, 5 have been chosen for the finals. Ravina is also a finalist. Do you remember her from St. Joseph's?'

'Yeah, she's so pretty too!'

She playfully nudged him.

'All this per age category?'

'Yeah. Also, another guy called Rahul. Anyway, so I did my slow rendition only, and the crowd seemed to really like it. But I think I need to talk to you about something else. I feel I have been having panic attacks. I freeze in some situations, and my heart starts beating fast. I get all sweaty and dizzy… And I also wanted to ask you what exactly is going on in your mind? It's obvious something is wrong, and you haven't spoken to me properly at all. And suddenly, Aarav is constantly talking to me, and I just cannot understand what is happening…' she ranted incessantly.

Dev was losing composure within. He so badly wanted to tell her that he is pretty sure he is developing feelings for her, but how could he? And now, what excuse was he supposed to give her? She would catch his lies. His mind was spiralling.

'Say something, no?'

'I'm actually thinking of joining the monastery, Alisha,' he blurted out.

'What? What are you talking about? What do you mean, join the monastery?' she asked completely blank. 'One of your new pranks, is it? Stop irritating me!'

'I'm talking about Dorje Drak. I'll explain more, but later, not now, please. I have a lot going on,' he whispered. He had absolutely no idea what he was talking about, but he was glad he got away from telling her the truth about how he felt.

He made such a serious face, Alisha was totally confused.

Chapter 6

Dorje Drak, also known as TDAC Nyingmapa Monastery, was located in Kasumpti Colony. It was a glorious 60-year-old Monastery in Panthaghati. It was proposed to be constructed in India by Kyabje Taklung Tsetrual Rinpoche when he moved to India from Tibet in the year 1959. It was set up with the help of the Indian Government. After the original monastery was demolished by the Chinese during their invasion of Tibet, Taklung Tsetrual Rinpoche decided to build it in Shimla. He was then the supreme head of the Nyingma School of Tibetan Buddhism.

Located just 6 km from the famous Mall Road, accessibility was easy. Nestled in the Himalayan foothills, it was architecturally rich and a famous pilgrimage spot. The scenic views surrounding the monastery added a unique charm – like a slice of heaven, a welcome refuge to every heart longing for peace.

Naina was an ardent devotee for a few years. She would frequently visit the monastery to meditate. She always went there to find parts of herself rejuvenated. Dev, being an avid reader and having a fine knowledge of various religions and cultures, found a deep connection with the place too. Their families even took a wonderful vacation a few years ago to Dharamshala, home to the Dalai Lama.

The 2 of them met the following morning to visit the monastery. They walked in silence to the meditation hall. Few onlookers stared at him. It was not often a young lad came in to meditate, unless of course they were already part of the Order. But for him, it was very normal. He had procured spiritual maturity at a young age, having visited many holy places and having read many children's renditions of different religions and cultures. They sat in contemplation for some time, after which they walked around the centre. As they were exiting, Naina excused herself to have a word with the Head of Administration. She had a keen desire to request a Samanera (young monk) to work in tandem with her findings on mental health and how spirituality can help one's mind in realising and anchoring the true purpose of life. He sat on the bench near the exit and saw with keen eyes the Lamas who were walking out of the meditation hall. The young men clad in their maroon robes, their inexplicable auras of peace and calm. He often wondered what it was like to be a part of them. To renounce worldly pleasures and attachments was definitely not easy. He never discussed this side of him with any of his family members or friends. Who would understand, anyway? He got up as he saw Naina coming in from a distance, and they walked out, the cold sun spraying its light on them.

'Come, let's get something to eat,' she said. They walked a few metres before they settled down in an old open-air restaurant with a lovely view of the city.

Chapter 7

They waited to satiate their hunger with the traditional cuisine of Thukpa, a warm bowl of noodle soup and vegetables. It was cold outside, and they had been awake since 6 am to visit the monastery. The atmosphere around Dorje Drak in the mornings was surreal. Snow-capped mountains in the backdrop cradled the beauty of the hermitage, with lush green trees and pristine blue skies protecting its legacy.

'I've been coming here since childhood... one of dad's close friend's relatives took the path of renunciation in the monastic order. Those days, dad would visit very frequently and bring us along with him. I really like it here. I'm surprised you asked me to bring you here. At your age, people have light interests in these places.'

'It is really nice. Well, yeah, maybe. But I like calm and quiet places. Since we were children, my parents have always emphasised the impact that spirituality can have on the human mind and soul. They worship many Gods & Goddesses yet have never forced us into any belief system. But I realise that is what intrigues people's minds. When you're left to follow any path, you will end up choosing what strikes a chord within you. But if it is forced upon you, you will automatically stay away from anything to prove a point. Look at Aarav and me, for instance; we are so different in our beliefs, yet we are deeply rooted in them.'

'That's true. Spirituality is an anchor. What is life without experiencing the divine connection anyway?'

'So true… but I cannot discuss this with many people. Very few people share the same wavelength.'

'Yeah, yeah, and you don't need to either. Anyway, how is Alisha? Are you still avoiding contact, or what?'

'Don't even ask. The other day, when I was with you, I was supposed to be at her rehearsals. She tried calling me repeatedly; I got to know when I went home. Aarav told me. It had totally slipped my mind when we were together. She also gets so upset; she wants me all the time, but she is literally getting close to him…I cannot understand? Isn't it strange? It was chaotic. Even my parents have been feeling I'm inattentive. So anyway, I went to meet her. She was very upset and asked me why I didn't come, etc. You know how I've told you about her? If something is on her mind, she will ask every question nonstop. It's cute undoubtedly, but tough to answer. So she upright asked me why I was being distant and all of that. And you will not believe what I've told her to avoid facing the truth of my feelings, which seem to have deepened ever since I opened up to you,' he said with a dejected expression.

'What did you tell her?' she asked curiously.

'I could not tell her that it bothers me right, with her sudden new equation with my brother. And if I make up something, she knows me too well and knows when I tend to be bizarre.'

'Yeah, ok, Dev, so what did you tell her?'

'I told her I want to join the monastery, and I was out with you that day.'

Naina's expression was completely blank for a few seconds. After that, she burst out laughing.

'Are you nuts? Where did that even come from? You are not even 18 yet. What is all this? And don't assume she believed you, please!'

'I don't think I gave her a chance to think about what I said. I was abrupt. Why, though, it isn't a bad idea, no?' He asked her pensively, his face between his hands.

'You have your studies, your career. Your life is in front of you. One love lost will not matter a few years down the line.'

'She is not one love to me, Naina. She is me,' he sounded hurt.

'I'm sorry, that isn't what I meant. I mean, you are too young to worry so much. Love comes and goes, even if you don't believe it right now. And how do you even know where this thing is going to go with your brother and Alisha? What about your medical degree? Have you thought about what your parents might have to say and what Aarav is going to do about it when he knows you may like Alisha too? He may just step back, right? And most importantly, this is not your age to make these decisions. You are being impulsive in your thoughts.' Naina went on worriedly.

'I never told you I'm going to do anything; God! I just said what I told Alisha as an excuse not to tell her how I feel!' he retorted.

She felt stupid. She kept quiet for a few minutes.

'But I know you from when you were younger... you wouldn't say something if you didn't have it on the back of your mind, and that scared me, I guess. I'm sorry.'

'Naina, I have never felt this way before. I am scared to meet her. It has been a friendship since childhood; I never imagined things being so different. And she is innocent; she is telling me everything she feels because she is innocent, and she is so close to me. If she has any idea I feel this way, she would also step back. But my point is, everything is going to change in either way. Either I have to step back for my sanity, or she will for hers. And I'm not ready for this change.'

'It is the only constant...'

She shrugged.

She didn't know what to say. They stared into the distance before the server asked them if there was anything else they would like to have. They asked for the bill and left the restaurant.

'Listen, how did your talk with the Samanera go?'

'He said it would be a long procedure. I need to fix appointments with the office and speak to the secretary. Let me see, I will look into it once I'm back,' she replied.

Chapter 8

If life were explained better, it would have been understood better.

'Breathe… Alisha,' she muttered to herself. She took deep breaths but was still palpitating. Beads of sweat wet her forehead, and she felt forlorn.

Anthony Sir was waiting for her to practice for the finals. Suddenly, ever since the selections were made, she began to dread the stage. When she had stepped on an hour earlier and the spotlight shone on her, she froze and could not sing at all. Tears streamed down her face, and she went behind the curtains feeling helpless. When sir and Rahul tried to ask her what was wrong, she didn't say anything. She asked them for a few minutes to get herself together.

She didn't know what to say. Nothing she could relate to or put a finger on was causing these feelings. They seemed like random mood swings, waves of panic that just engulfed her from time to time.

The previous night, she had not slept well. Aarav had called her at 10 pm.

'Why is he calling this late, Al?' Aunty Asha asked her, surprised and annoyed. She was very fond of both the brothers, but she never understood or approved of late night phone calls, spending excessive time with someone, and all of that. Arun, her husband, was a more relaxed man.

'I have no idea, Mum. Let me speak to him.' She didn't seem to realise her mum's irritation at the time.

'They are teenagers, Ashu. Please don't be a hawk around them unless you do not want to know what is happening in their lives. If you keep asking so many questions, she won't answer truthfully anyway.'

'What nonsense!' she snapped. 'There is something called discipline. This is not the time to call and chat.'

'So, what do you want him to do? Call her in the middle of the day and express his feelings?'

'Huh? What are you talking about? What feelings? Alisha would have told me if there was something. Besides, I don't think she is like that as a person…' Asha aunty went on, denial being a comforting feeling.

'What is that type of person, Ashu? The kind who doesn't have feelings?' He enjoyed cornering her in arguments. 'What type of person doesn't have feelings?' He found it funny how his wife tried to deny what was obvious. 'What type of person is that, tell me also… must be a special kind, no?' he went on with a smirk in his voice.

They raced along for a while. He knew the look in Alisha's eyes and told Asha how he felt – that either he liked her, or she liked him, or something was going on between those 2. He wondered, too, if it would affect her bond with Dev. Somewhere at the back of his mind, he always envisioned them together on that blue bench... It was funny to think of it with Aarav.

'They are still young. They won't take anything too seriously now.'

In the dark hall, Alisha switched on the night lamp by her phone and sank into the maroon sofa.

'Why are you calling me so late? Is it important?' she spoke in a soft voice. Her long hair was flowing over her shoulders. 'One minute,' she said and tied her hair into a bun before he could answer. She was nervous for the rehearsal the next day.

'Of course it is important,' Aarav said flatly.

She waited for him to explain.

'I don't know how to do this, Alisha, but since you have asked me directly, I think I should answer you honestly. I really like you. I have been thinking about you all the time, day and night. When I'm with you, I don't know what to say. But when I'm not with you, I'm always having conversations with you in my head. I don't know how you feel about me, but this is how I feel. I want you to be mine,' Aarav spoke without a pause.

She was stunned for a few moments, she didn't know what to say.

'You there?'

'But... but Aarav, don't take this the wrong way. You have felt like this for other girls also, before me... right? I mean, obviously, you have. What I am trying to say is that it happens often to you… and then you keep jumping in and out of relationships. I don't mean this in a bad way, so please don't misunderstand me, but I don't think I'm made like that at all.'

'That's being rude. My brother tells you all sorts of things. What do you mean jumping in and out?! Makes me sound like a monkey!'

She laughed.

'We have known each other since we were little. Dev and I never discuss you. *(That was a lie, they only discussed him of late)* Saloni and Priya, whom you had liked a year ago, both of them were my friends too. I got a lot of scoop on you, haha! Anyway, I'm not saying anything to hurt you. I'm just saying, I don't know if you *feel* this way or if you *think* you feel this way. And I don't know how I feel either. There are layers to me you don't even know, maybe once you do, you will feel differently.'

'That's for me to decide. Besides, please don't do the thinking for me.'

Alisha sensed the undertone of impatience. 'Think about it instead of getting snappy. I don't mean to be rude. I just don't want to get into something… you know… just to get out of it. I'm kind of old school. Once I'm involved in something, I would prefer to just be in it, unless something crazy happens, obviously!'

'That means you have already been thinking about us' he said.

She blushed pink in the warm glow of the night lamp.

'Good night now! I have an early morning rehearsal tomorrow.'

'Yeah, Dev was telling me. Good luck.'

After they hung up, she was wondering when to tell Dev about all of this. The boy never seemed to be around anymore, and when he did, he was always so preoccupied and flippant. One part of her was giddy with excitement, butterflies in her stomach, a heart racing and blushing with a new love found. The other part of her felt like the ground was slowly and surely slipping away from her feet, a secure blanket not around to discuss every minute feeling, without questioning its significance or relevance. With Dev, every part of her felt important. Lost in thought, she kept playing different scenarios in her head until she fell asleep.

Chapter 9

*The essence is to create a reality for yourself
where you are happy.*

Dev was busy doodling, writing quotes, and changing lines of his poetry instead of doing his assignment in the library. He was too preoccupied with random thoughts. It was a childhood hobby, and a good one, he often thought. It was like a safe space for him; whenever he didn't know what step to take next, this pastime of his kept him busy until new ideas came to him.

Next year, he would start his medical degree at the prestigious IGMC. He had sorted out his hostel accommodation and all the formalities. When he was younger, he always thought Aarav would be a doctor of some sort, and he always followed that thought process, but as they grew up… things were so different. Aarav was more cut out for the corporate sector, as he was a people's person.

Dev had developed a profound interest in biochemistry, which began at a career counselling fair a year ago. The combinations of different drugs had given way to different cures, but he wanted to research on how to cut down the side effects of these drugs, to give the cure but not at the cost of such harsh side effects. Apart from the analysis of blood and body fluids to measure the levels of various substances, he wanted to research how to reduce the drug composition so as to reduce side effects, while not compromising on the quality of the remedy.

'the echo still stings... no, no... resonance...'

Trapped in a treasurr... hmm... treasury? Olden? No, antique...

He was daydreaming while thinking of his lines in the library, while Harsh was trying to make eye contact. 'Dev!' he was trying to aim small paper planes at him. He finally looked up. Harsh pointed at his watch and signalled to leave.

'What are you always daydreaming about, bro?'

'Nothing, man, was just bored.'

'Do I confirm with the boys for next Saturday, doubles?' Harsh asked about their regular tennis game.

'No, not Saturday. It's Alisha's finals. I need to be there,' he grimaced.

'Why aren't you excited? You have been helping her practice for ages.'

'No, no, I am excited. Fingers crossed!'

'So, when do we play the doubles?'

'I'll update you, maybe sometime next week? Got to run now! I'll see you in the evening for a game.'

He walked past the bridge across the long, lush acres of their school campus. He had a tonne of studies to finish in the next few weeks. With the medical entrance approaching, he had little time to do anything else. He went home and straight to his room. Since the events of the last few weeks, he tried his best to avoid Alisha. One night, his mum sat with him, asking him if he was okay. He had been unusually quiet, joined guitar coaching amidst the other things he had to do, and seemed indifferent. He assured her he was just busy with his studies.

The thing that made him the most uncomfortable was when Aarav questioned him about being distant from her. He could not get his head around the change in their equation. It was always *Dev & Alisha*, knowing every little and big detail of each other's minds, fears, fantasies, and realities, so when he realised that she started expressing herself to Aarav instead of him, it pierced through him and his identity. The blue bench seldom saw them; it was a slow realisation for Dev that maybe this is what love felt like, but it went out of his reach even before he acknowledged it.

They would sit for hours together jamming on different mash-ups. She would practice all her songs with him. He was with her through every competition she took part in since she began. Her every sentiment, laugh, and tear belonged to him. He tried to envision a scenario of things being the same. So what if Aarav and she fall in love? It is not going to change anything in their friendship, right? He tried to convince himself, but then why was he feeling so helpless? As he continued to sort out his stuff around him and listened to music, Passenger's 'Let Her Go' was playing on the music player. It was their favourite song to do together. He didn't like to sing, but she would always get her way with him. That's when it hit him that he was hopelessly in love, and it hurt so badly because he had to let her go.

Chapter 10

The hardest battles are the ones fought in silence.

Alisha stared into the mirror; she was wearing her knee-length black dress. She combed her long hair neatly as she rehearsed her song softly, her throat itching. The song she chose for the finals was 'It's all coming back to me now' by Celine Dion. It was one of her favourite songs, and the range was beautiful to be able to do her own version. She tried to take a deep breath, but she coughed; the tension crept through her. *This was not the day to feel ill.* The competition was 8 hours away and an hour-long drive from school. With quivering fingers, she picked up her phone to dial Dev's home... it was Aarav who answered instead.

'Hey, hi!' she croaked.

'Hey, you! Why do you sound so different? Are you okay, sweetheart?'

She felt goose bumps, butterflies, and nausea all at once.

'I'm not feeling too well! Are you guys coming for the show? Where is Dev?' she spoke rapidly.

Aarav never seemed to worry when she and Dev hung out, but of late, he was always curious. It was probably because they had been close since childhood. He had not officially discussed his feelings towards her with his younger brother;

that would be so weird. But nevertheless, it was unspoken and understood. Communication between siblings is not something everyone can boast about.

'Yes, we are coming. How would we miss it? He has gone to play tennis; he will come home in a while. Do I pass on a message? All okay with the practice?'

Alisha was stumped. She didn't know what to say. She had developed an attraction towards Aarav, so she didn't want to portray herself as vulnerable. It was too soon in what was the infancy of their relationship, if she could call it that. But with Dev, oh dear! How she longed for him to come on the line and just talk or not talk, it wouldn't matter. He would be there to give her the support she needed, in words or in silence.

'No, it's all good! I'll see you later, then!'

'Hey, good luck. I'm sure you're going to be wonderful tonight!'

'Don't put pressure, Aru!' she flinched.

'It's called encouragement... never mind...' His voice trailed off.

There was a knock on her door, and she opened it to find her parents standing there with a little bouquet of pink chrysanthemums. She hugged them both and felt emotional.

'We're so proud of you, love.'

'Mum, dad...'

Alisha couldn't find her voice. Everything started feeling like a whirlwind. She sat on the edge of her bed; she could hear her heart thumping. Her back was wet, and she felt frail in her arms; she could hear her parents talking but could not understand a word. Everything was a loud blur.

Her mother was worried and went to get her a glass of water. She took a wet cloth and dabbed her forehead gently. After a few moments, she felt better.

'Sorry'.

'Are you nervous? Because it's normal to be,' she held her hand.

'Alisha, what is happening? Are you having panic attacks? It seems that way to me, since a month or 2 now.'

No one spoke in the room.

'Don't over-analyse or feel it's taboo to talk to me. I have had these too. And the symptoms you are experiencing, I have been noticing this for a while now. I didn't want to say anything until I was sure.'

Asha hushed him. This was not the time to discuss all this. A couple of hours before the competition, they could speak about all this later. Alisha was already overwhelmed… she sunk onto the floor corner… Softly sobbing, her arms crossed over her knees. She needed a hug and something to drink, not a long talk.

'Come here, baby.' Asha held Alisha close as she signaled to Arun to not discuss anything at that moment. He went out to give them a couple of minutes.

'Listen, chin up, and speak to us,' said Arun when he got back into the room.

'I'm just really scared for tonight. I have been preparing for months, but today my voice seems gruff, and I have a sore throat. I don't want to attend this! And even on a personal front, I have been a wreck. Aarav has been in touch with me very often for a few weeks, but Dev seems to be growing distant. I can't help but feel guilty. I'm getting a strong vibe that he is not okay with this, but he is never around me anymore to have a proper conversation. And yes, I have been experiencing these symptoms for a while now… I know I should have mentioned something earlier,' she rambled on.

They sat together, conversing for half an hour before deciding to seek professional help shortly. Sometime later, Dev finally showed up. She was a lot better than an hour ago and was able to tell him the entire episode.

'What is it? Tell me. Why do you avoid me so much these days? You are not okay with Aarav and me getting closer, I know... it's something to do with that, right?'

He flipped his hair the other way and shrugged. 'No, Al. Why would you assume something so silly? We have both been so busy, haven't we? How would that make any difference to us being friends? I'm just preoccupied with the entrance exams no. I'm finding it so difficult and questioning my choices!' He was good with lies.

'A part of me knows you are lying.'

'Come on now, practice a bit. All that crying has made your voice all gruff,' he teased.

'Look, I even learnt how to play this on the guitar so you could practice with me.' The little things he did for her touched her heart always.

She was so thrilled, but her voice was indeed strange today. He worried about her.

'Listen, just rest a while. You have time, and whatever it is, it'll be okay. Imagine how amazing a feat you have achieved by getting selected for a state-wide singing competition! Very few people get to live their dreams, and it is okay to struggle a bit; that's what makes it worth the while, isn't it?'

'Yeah, but it shouldn't be like it's turning into my nightmare!' she retorted.

She heard the doorbell and went towards it when Dev gave her a piece of paper. 'Here, read this…'

'What is it?'

'I completed *The Guitar*, finally!'

'Oh my gosh, really?'

It was a piece of poetry Dev had been working on for months but couldn't finish. They had a bet that if he finished it before her competition, he could ask her for anything, and she couldn't refuse! It was their childlike way of motivating each other…

They hugged each other tightly, and she promised to read it that night.

'When are you going to ask me for what you want?' she asked, curiously.

I don't think you will be able to give me what I want, he thought to himself.

'Soon!' he smiled.

A few minutes later, some more of her friends gathered at her place. Some brought greeting cards to wish her luck, while the others brought food, flowers, and what not! There was a small bouquet with yellow and white daisies, and a small card on it. She was wondering who it was from. Her mum opened it and had a big smile! It was from Anthony Sir on behalf of the academy, wishing her luck. 'Glad you found your style, have fun while singing!' it had said.

She was excited to see so much love and positivity. She felt so loved and encouraged. But deep inside her stomach, she was so scared to disappoint everyone who was rooting for her. She had to give it her best. The Voice of Himachal was not an easy contest to be a part of, and the selection process had been so rigorous. The tension was mounting inside her as she sat in the bus and headed for the famous Gaiety Heritage Complex.

She went to the registration counter and finished the formalities. She took her token number and had the badge pinned onto her black dress. Alisha looked gorgeous in her black dress with her long brown hair cascading over her shoulders. She had lined her lower eyes and put on a subtle shade of pink lipstick with her mum's help. She didn't know much about make-up but she felt pretty and radiant. She had sipped on warm ginger tea and tried to calm her nerves. She had come this far, and now she had to just give it her best. Her fellow contestants were all seated in the dressing room, discussing the songs they were going to sing.

Chapter 11

The ability to take perspective is unique to a few minds. Those who learn it see life as a whole spectrum; the rest can just see one colour at a time.

The auditorium was huge, with a capacity of over 3000 people. The Voice of Himachal was an annual singing competition which was held here. Having a few different age groups and other criteria, the contestants were finally shortlisted, and thirty of them were chosen. It was good for a three-hour show, not too long and not too short either, with the results being announced in the last half-hour segment. Winners from this contest often went on to participate in national level competitions, or if some were lucky and got enough publicity, they were part of television ads, short films, and so on. They also got exposure to music companies whom they could record their labels under, if it worked out.

The backstage was bustling with vibes of positivity, enthusiasm, nervousness, and excitement. The ushers in the front looked elegant in their white and black outfits, guiding the audience to their places. The Chief Guest for the evening was Mrs. Lulu Francis, a veteran singer from the age of 12, with one too many accolades to her name. She was a great inspiration not only to the state of Himachal Pradesh but to India.

When Alisha heard that Mrs. Lulu was going to be the chief guest, she was overjoyed and nervous! She had such a lovely voice, and more than that, she was such a fine lady. Alisha remembered the speech Mrs. Lulu had given on television one day when she had won the award for the best singer in the Original Composition category. Mrs. Lulu had written a song on India's fight for freedom, and the lyrics had touched every member of the audience. It was hands down the best song of that day. When she had won, she took the centre stage to express her immense gratitude to the people who helped make a difference in her journey and in her accomplishments, and she concluded by saying, 'Making one's country proud is no mean feat. One should never compare their accomplishments or achievements to others, but to their own capacity. It all starts within us, when we light the fire because even a small flame, when lit, can erase the dark. And there is no greater privilege than being given an opportunity to make your country proud, in whichever field it may be.'

The emcee had welcomed the guests and entertained them with casual repartee, and the show was about to begin. The contestants were being called on one by one, and the audience cheered for everyone. Being picked in random order, Rahul went first. He did really well by singing Michael Jackson's 'Heal the World.' Even though common, it was a fantastic song to choose to showcase his vocal range.

The auditorium was filled with the melodious sounds of different voices, and Alisha's turn was next. As her name was called, she walked slowly to the podium. Yes, she really needed to consult professional help. It was now that she realised that she could hear her heartbeat louder than the crowd that was cheering. She could barely see the people sitting; everyone was a blur, and she was perspiring. Part of her wanted to run away and hide, but in no way could she now back out. She closed her eyes to say a prayer and went on to begin. The spotlight shone on her. The sound of the piano calmed her nerves, and she began singing. She started beautifully, especially the first chorus. *Celine Dion would probably enjoy this performance,* she thought. She looked beautiful, and her family was ecstatic. They were all so excited to see her up there, living her passion, realizing her dream.

Dev and Aarav sat between their friends. Dev was mesmerised. Aarav cheered softly, but something seemed off. When Dev tried to talk to him, Aarav was stammering and a tad bit incoherent, but Dev didn't pay too much attention to him. He was enjoying the show thoroughly. And that's when it happened.

Alisha's voice broke.

She had not managed to carry on, she had coughed and tried to control it, and resume, but what followed was silent chaos. Her voice refused to cooperate, and the background singers quickly increased their volume so as to not make it obvious, and somehow she managed to complete the remaining 2 minutes. Her parents looked worried, but they kept calm. It was Dev who ran out of the auditorium. Aarav stayed put for a while; he was stunned at what happened. Anna urged him to go backstage so he could meet her and check on her in the waiting room... while the show continued.

Chapter 12

Failure is success turned upside down.

Back in the dressing room, Alisha just sat down. The management helped her with some water and made sure she was relaxed. She didn't react much; she seemed numb, staring blankly at the wall. She could hear the voices of her fellow contestants, the crowd, and the music fading and restarting in the background.

She clipped her hair and tried to remove the kohl from under her eyes. She searched for her bag to find the paper Dev had given her. She fumbled for a while before she found it, and as she began reading, she tried to disconnect from what had just happened...

'Deep inside the woods, I hear the sound of strings,
A hundred years of a mystic past, the resonance still
stings...
Trapped in an antique treasury, filled with mistakes and
dust,
I take out my guitar, now completely rust...
Raw ancient sounds, filled with nostalgia of sin,
An uncertain harmony, a strange desire to win,
I play my guitar amidst a forest of green trees,
In spite of knowing it all, a song of threatening mysteries.
A fire burning, a scintillating old time,

Playing new words to the same old rhyme,
Tribes in dusky light dance around flames that fume,
I furiously play my guitar to the same old tune.
Downpours in the village, skies in fury,
I place my guitar back in the treasury,
Abusing the winds, the sound is lost in bliss,
It's not my guitar, it's the tune I miss…
I run from my tent, back outside,
Away from my guitar, wet forests have dried…
But sometimes, deep inside the woods, I still hear the
sound of strings,
Of a hundred years, of a mystic past, the resonance still
stings.'

What a brilliant piece of work, she thought. Someone from the team came up to her.

'Alisha, someone is waiting outside the door to speak with you.'

Alisha did not want to face anybody, but she could not convey that to anyone either. She reluctantly walked towards the exit. It was Aarav standing at the door, half-smiling. Her heart sank; she thought Dev would be the one standing. She was angry with him, but angrier with herself. What was she getting close to Aarav for when she wanted Dev to talk to all the time? What was this double-sided emotional drama that she was getting herself into?

'Hey!' He leaned in to hug her. She fell into his embrace. 'Are you ok?' He seemed concerned. *How would she be okay? She literally had a debacle on stage. What a stupid question, she thought to herself.* Standing so close to him, she could smell his breath, and it had the faint smell of something she could not recognise. She could pretend with him; he didn't know her inside out, at least not yet, and in some twisted way, Alisha felt safe pretending. She knew once she was alone, she would be enveloped with feelings of failure.

'I'm fine, I think. I don't know, Aru. I kind of saw this coming. I was feeling unwell earlier in the day. I was dreading it, actually.' She could not bring herself to admit how hollow and mortified she felt. This was her dream tumbling down like a waterfall, and she was going wherever it took her.

Aarav stepped back and looked into her eyes. 'It is okay to be vulnerable with me, you know. There is no need to pretend. I know how important this is to you. It was just a bad day. Please don't ever let it ruin your confidence. Your voice is absolutely beautiful.'

She was touched. It was too big a moment to digest what had happened back there, but it felt nice to be reassured. They held hands and stepped out for a few minutes. It was cold, and it felt like it would rain any second. Just behind the dressing room was a small porch with wooden benches. They sat close to each other. They could feel the raindrops on their clothes. Aarav leaned in closer and held her face in his hands; he pulled her closer and kissed her lips gently. His fingers were entwined in her hair, her neck swaying to the movements of his hands. Alisha closed her eyes and was completely lost in a trance. She didn't know if she felt the same for him, or was she merely trying to escape her feelings about her failure. Thoughts of Dev crowded her mind, but she was too dazed to understand what was going on around her. They kissed for a long time, long enough to realise they were completely drenched and could hear people calling Alisha's name. They quickly got up and tried to look around to make sure no one saw them.

As they walked back all the way to the front of the dressing room, her family and friends were all waiting to see if she was okay. She was careful not to breakdown. She held herself together and told them she would wind up along with her fellow contestants, head held high. Her throat hurt; it was so sore. She didn't know what to focus on in that moment.

At the back of her mind, she kept wondering where Dev was. It was very unlikely of him to just disappear on her in that moment. She was going to have a long talk with him and clear things out. What sort of friendship was this when he wasn't there with her at her darkest moment?

As everyone dispersed into their respective places, the rain had soaked Dev who had witnessed Alisha and Aarav on the bench. He was the first one to come, but Aarav had requested him to let him speak to her first. He walked a long distance before getting a ride home. After that, he didn't meet Alisha for days together. He tried avoiding her as much as he could. She tried a lot to get in touch with him, but he would always get away with a quick hi and bye. Being in the final year of high school was different from their younger years. They had different subjects and different timings, and that made it easier to get away.

He was never there at the recreation centre for a game of tennis, nor was he there in the building when they would usually meet for a walk. He did his best to elude her. Alisha, on the other hand, kept longing and waiting for the conversation to happen. When she didn't find him there after her biggest moment of failure, she was convinced things had changed to a large extent. She hid the emotions deep inside and didn't process any of it; it was evident that he was intentionally staying away. When they did manage to cross paths, he would make small talk and leave from there. It was obvious now, but she still hoped. She felt selfish, wanting the best of both of them, but she didn't think things through. If she knew what would happen with Dev and her friendship, she probably would never have let Aarav into her life so deeply.

In the meantime, she got closer to Aarav. They spent all their time together, stealing kisses wherever they could. He wooed her from morning until night. She felt conscious of her body, of her thoughts, but she could not bring herself to tell him about the tremors, the palpitations... what the doctor had identified as chronic anxiety the week before. No, that was not something she could tell him just yet.

Aarav paid little attention to the fact that Alisha and Dev were not close friends anymore. He did not realise the drift that was caused. He was falling deeply in love with her. He was the perfect boyfriend, always surprising her. Aarav did not know how to express himself verbally, but he was always there to make her heart skip a beat. The attraction between the 2 of them escalated, and Alisha found herself questioning her tender beliefs when she was with him. He was 21, and she was 18; the world didn't matter around them. Their love was bursting in flames that thrived even in the snow. But Aarav too was hiding something from Alisha, rather, from himself. Every evening after their rendezvous, he would go to his old classmate Akshay's hostel to drink, smoke, and get lost in the dark world of substances, unfamiliar to him.

PART TWO

Chapter 1

*Nothing is more important than safeguarding
one's mental health.*

'Aarav, let's go,' Dev was irritated.

He just stood there, blank, near the exit of the rehabilitation premises at the IGMC campus.

'You are going to be fine. You just have to follow their instructions.'

That was the one thing Aarav would not do. No one could understand what was going on with him. He was like a whole new person, and not in a good way.

Dev was pretty flustered. When he looked back at the last few years, it seemed like he was only filled with regret. Alisha and Aarav weren't the correct match for each other. He wished he had intervened at the right moment… what had started out as a fire of passion between the 2 of them had burned them out completely. They were led to the darkest places within themselves. And he was constantly dangling between the 2, trying to help them, being helpless himself.

<u>**Six years ago**</u>

'Come on, bro. It is her 20th birthday, and yours too, a week prior. Let me do something special for the both of you, no?'

Aarav was coaxing Dev, who was completely against the idea.

'You do it for her, please. You know I'm not a fan of these get-togethers. It sounds so ridiculous, like we are kids waiting for a party!'

'Well, you never had a problem earlier. What is it, man? Do you *still* have a problem that she and I are dating?' he asked his younger brother for the nth time.

'First of all, when did I tell you I have a problem? I have no clue why you keep asking anyway. No, I do not have a problem. Does she know about your excessive drinking and smoking? You're playing her so sensibly. That is my problem. Making me also lie to her. It's been more than a year since you have been living this dual life with her. I've known her all my life, and closely. She will be angry as hell when she knows you are hiding it from her to this addicted extent. And when mum and dad get to know, you will be in big trouble,' he snapped. 'And then she will be furious that I didn't tell her, blah, blah, such stupid drama because you just want to lie, so mature, man!'

'Look, you don't need to interfere in that part of my life. I'm asking you something else. Don't change the topic and be stupid.'

'Are you nuts?!' he exclaimed. 'Dude, she and I do not talk as often anymore. Yeah, we remain the best of friends and all that jazz, but our routines and priorities have changed. The last thing we both would want is a joint party. We are not in school anymore Aarav! Every time you're suggesting some nonsense.' He ranted.

'Thanks and sorry, I appreciate your gesture. But it is not what I want. You know I don't relate to all this. And just to let you know, by you being intoxicated with different substances, it is going to really mess with your work, more importantly, your health. Dad is bound to find out because your Company Head has already sent a warning letter home stating that if your productivity decreases, they will need you to serve a three-month notice period and quit. You will have to put down your papers, Aru! They have already mentioned that you have taken more leaves than you were allowed to, so there is a salary deduction as well.

'I did not want to mention it to you; I was home when the post came. If it continues, they will make calls. Please, think things through.'

'I only drink at night. Smoking during the day doesn't count for intoxication.'

'Smoking ganja does.'

Dev continued. 'How do you even know if you love someone, if you like your job, if you are doing the maximum that you can each day, if you are never in your senses? Like, how do you perceive the quality of your life if you're not sober, like, ever? And if you are so confident about your lifestyle, why are you afraid to tell Alisha, mum, and dad about it? Why do you hide it from them? You know why, Aarav? It is because **you know** that none of them will have your back, none of them will buy into your crap. You know what you are doing is dangerous. And being so close to Alisha, you have put me in a position where I am feeling guilty because I always protect her. How do I protect her from you, Aarav?

I know this will lead to a disaster. Why don't you get it? And when she knows that I knew, she will never talk to me again. Get real, for once. This is not you, stop believing in this façade you have created, please!'

Aarav was adjusting his hair with gel while his brother was hysterically trying to explain to him that he was voluntarily putting his hand into a fire. He did feel a faint tinge of fear, but he was quick to dismiss it from his mind.

'Get a life... don't be such a nag! Shouldn't have even asked you about the birthday nonsense. Bye!' With that, he slammed the door and left to meet his friends.

It had been more than a year since Aarav had been going out of line. But he was also very sneaky; he made it seem to Alisha that he was a chiller, someone who would show her the fun side of life. She didn't have an inkling that he was neck-deep into these habits, let alone once in a while. It was such a sad change in him, Dev thought. He is charming and intelligent, and because of bad company, he was always looking for loopholes in his day to experience alcohol and drugs. It was rather scary, and Dev, being in the medical field, felt all the more worried and responsible for his brother. He tried telling him to cut back, but Aarav never paid attention to him. He was happy in his bliss and felt like he had everything under control. For Dev, this was a bigger excuse to run away from her because every time they met, he felt he was deceiving her. His brother was not the kind of mate she was looking for, and he couldn't even expose him. He really missed her; they did meet. But things were not the same. It felt superficial and platonic, and they both didn't do a great job pretending.

Chapter 2

A clear conscience can be masked by substances.

Aarav kissed her gently, and then frantically, and then he kissed her gently again. They were behind a tree by the lakeside, in a quiet corner where nobody could see them. It was late in the evening, and the lake shimmered with reflections of the scattered moonlight.

'Anthony Sir called my parents today… to ask me to resume my vocal training,' she whispered. 'I didn't have it in me to speak to him on the phone, but I'll go to the studio soon, I was thinking.'

This phase was new and exhilarating for her. She had never experienced this kind of intimacy before. She was still figuring out how she felt, and he made her feel calm, safe, comfortable, beautiful, and loved. It was a great distraction from her thoughts for the most part.

'So, resume it. Come on, sweetheart. You know it was because of your inflamed throat that you lost the competition. It has been a year. You surely can't give up on your talent, your dreams, right?' He held her tight. 'These things are bound to happen; setbacks are a part of growth.'

'It is not that, Aarav. I don't feel bad that I lost. Winning and losing are part of it, and really, that is not what bothered me. But that day, standing in front of such a big crowd, my voice just stopped. It was scary. And also, I don't have the confidence to restart after that day. I don't know if I can muster up the courage. There is also something else I want to tell you, but maybe not now...' Her voice trailed away. *How do I say I get panic attacks and not sound silly*? She thought to herself.

She spoke again. 'Listen, I think we need to tell our parents about us. It's been almost a year now, and I usually don't keep information so deep from them. I feel guilty and awkward around them. Maybe it is different for you, but for me, I am the only child. Besides, we always talk to each other about our personal lives. It's like they already know, but I'm not admitting it, which is kind of dumb. They know we are so close; my dad suspects it all the time. It's high time I acknowledge it to them...'

Aarav withdrew. He had told her from the start not to tell her parents anything in detail, and that made her very uncomfortable. She finally decided to speak to him about it. 'Why don't we give it some time, sweetheart? Don't you think it is too soon? We both don't know what the future looks like....'

'A year and counting is not too soon Aarav. They are my parents; they are like my friends. I do not like the feeling that they do not know the biggest thing about my life, Aru. I don't think I can carry on this disguise anymore. They're not stupid, and I don't see any reason to hide. Whether there is a future or not is secondary right now. I have to be honest with them anyway.'

'If you tell them, there will be questions, there will be expectations,' he sounded disappointed, like a fairy tale would end.

'So, what? We need to figure out what we want anyway. We can't be without direction any longer. I'm pretty sure I'm telling them, and you need to figure out what you want to do. If it gets serious, then so be it. If there are questions, we need to answer them. If there are expectations, we need to see what works for us and what doesn't.' He knew he didn't have a choice after that conversation, and she was happy with the clarity she was able to give him post her doctors visit.

They began walking towards the lakeside. Hand in hand, they strolled until they reached the restaurant. They met Harsh, Anna, and the rest of the group for dinner.

All of their friends knew they were a couple now. Anna was secretly heartbroken. She and Aarav were very close, and she always thought Aarav fancied her, hoping he would ask her out soon. When she saw them together, she realised maybe she was imagining it all along.

But that is exactly who Aarav was – everyone who met him felt special and loved. He was enthusiastic, giving, and very desirable. *The only thing he didn't have was perspective, and that is something she would know much later.*

But he was attracted to Alisha because she didn't perceive him the way other girls did. Alisha looked at him like Dev's blah elder brother. She had seen him grow from his stroppy moustache days to the mature, chiselled jawline that he had now. With her, he felt like he could be any version of himself and still be desired. He initially wondered if he had come in between their friendship because certain changes are just that obvious. But Dev obviously denied it, and Alisha never seemed to acknowledge that aspect. She didn't know him well enough to bring it up with him yet; she didn't have the right questions for what would surely be wrong answers. It was a delicate place, so she never went there with him. Those thoughts slowly became whiffs in the air, and with that, he subdued his own opinions on it.

Chapter 3

To give someone hope is a privilege.

'So, how exactly do you define mental health?' asked Dr Amar. 'It's okay to be nervous. You can share your views nevertheless.'

She was perspiring, it had become a hobby of her mind. She was jumpy.

'I guess it is by being positive at all times, giving the best that you can to every given situation,' she spoke fast, hoping this appointment that her parents insisted on would get over in that very instant.

Her parents had set her up for an hour-long session with a renowned psychiatrist in the city. It was hard to find a well-known recommendation. The topic of mental health was such that nobody wanted to discuss it freely. The fact that they went to see a counsellor or a psychiatrist was, sadly, still taboo.

But, thankfully, it was Dev who got them the recommendation. Who else could it be! He had got the contact from Naina. Alisha's family was very particular that Dev didn't divulge any details to anyone. He had to be tactful. But with the constant panic attacks she was facing, her family did not want to ignore it. After reading about it, her father, Arun, even spoke to some office colleagues just to discuss it as a topic and was wondering if people responded to it, but he didn't get much information.

It was Asha aunty who approached Dev. She knew Naina's field of study through them, and she also knew Alisha opened up about everything to Dev. Alisha had once told them that she felt like a fish out of water. For no apparent reason, she would break into a sweat, her heartbeat would be so loud she could hear it, and she would feel a mental blur in whatever task she took up… even digesting food had become a huge problem.

Dev had insisted that they discuss it with her parents right away. Of late, they didn't communicate as much. With the new dynamics between the 3 of them, it was rather complicated in her head. But this was important, and she could always count on him.

Naina was more than happy to recommend Dr Amar to them. His work in the field of counselling psychiatry was remarkable, and he had positively impacted many people's lives.

'No, no, my dear… that would be so pressurising. You have it all wrong…' he smiled. Adjusting his spectacles on his nose, he continued, 'Mental health is not about being perfect. It is much like physical health. It needs tending, it needs love and care. You need to be careful about what you feed your mind and how you use your time. It is like what you would do when you get a stomach ache or a headache; you cannot force it to go away. You would rest, eat light, and take appropriate medication, and so on.

'The very same way, mental health needs to be cared for. The sad part about it is, people are scared to talk about it. Admitting to someone that you are scared, paranoid, angry, frustrated, or any such negative emotion these days has become taboo. People are judgemental, and it has become a vicious circle. Perfection is just a mirage. But you cannot blame them; it all starts because no one wants to address an emotion with empathy, compassion, and practicality. People are striving to be perfect, but what sort of perfection exists? Can your body be free of a headache, toothache, a tummy ache? If the body is not spared of physical problems, how can the mind be free? It is natural, but no one wants to understand. And that suppression of emotions is what leads to people taking wrong steps in their lives.

'Let me simplify it for you.'

He noticed she was waiting to just run away, but he was used to it. It took time for patients to adapt and think on a deeper level.

His words were slow, crisp, and impactful. 'Almost every one of us is prone to experiencing mental health issues. If you have a mind, you will definitely be predisposed to feeling and living through different emotions. **The idea is to cultivate emotional regulation and the ability to not suppress oneself.** You firstly need to know *that there is nothing wrong in what you are going through.* Secondly, *there are techniques to improve the state of mind you find yourself in,* and thirdly, *prescribed medication is an option only when necessary.* The root cause is often related to one's repressed emotions in some instances. On a broader perspective, the aim is to help you be self-reliant without putting pressure on yourself, and that begins by practising self-acceptance.

'It is something that some people experience in 2 aspects – so I need you to guide me on that. It could be purely psychological, physiological, or a mix of both. *There are layers to our mind. It's the effort you take to connect the dots that will start making sense to you.* And for that, I need your help to please note down what you feel triggers these attacks in you. It can be situational; it can be a memory. For now, I am putting you on a very mild muscle relaxant to help you cope with the day-to-day distress.'

'Thank you very much, doctor'...she mumbled nervously, hoping this was the end of their meeting. She was relieved and wanted to run away, but it didn't get to be so easy. She wasn't able to absorb the information all at once.

Her parents were ushered in to describe and explain more about what she was feeling, in their opinion. Since she wasn't able to explain much of it on her own, with their inputs, Dr Amar got a rough idea that she had acute anxiety. In his opinion, he felt it could be more psychological, but he needed to know her family history to arrive at a proper diagnosis and treatment. However, he did recommend an hour of counselling every week for the next 3 months.

She felt sort of stranded; there was nothing in her life that justified her feeling this way. She didn't know when or how this whole thing became a big part of her personality, but it was increasingly difficult to concentrate on school work, singing, and even the basics of her routine. She found comfort and distraction in Aarav's company.

While leaving the doctor's clinic, she finally confided in her parents that Aarav and she were dating. Her mum was quite taken aback, but her dad knew it all along.

'Just be careful, baby. He may be a charming boy, but do not make any decisions right now. And please, don't get involved in the heat of the moment.'

Her mother didn't say anything; she didn't want to impose her fears on her daughter, especially since she had taken the step to tell them about it.

Chapter 4

Over the next few days, Alisha woke up feeling less tense and more relaxed. It was a new sensation for her. It had been a while since she woke up looking forward to the day. She realised over the following days that the pills were taking effect. But she didn't get harsh on herself, she was just so grateful that she was not feeling low anymore. She felt calm and composed and that was amazing. She showered, got dressed, and went to the kitchen to spend time with her mum, who was pleasantly surprised to see her little girl in a happy mood, not stressing and huffing.

They chatted for a while, and though she had some big decisions to make regarding college, she first went to the institute to meet Anthony Sir. Aarav was to join her after that to have lunch.

'Hello!' Sir spoke with a bright smile. 'Finally, you came! How can you just disappear on me?'

'I'm so sorry, Sir! After that fiasco on stage, I really lacked the confidence to come back.'

'These things are stepping stones, Alisha. I understand completely, but an important lesson that everyone should learn is that it is **_OKAY_** to fail. In fact, the more we see failure, the more humble we become, and the deeper our ability to garner inner strength.'

He went on. 'Yes, of course, when we work hard, we want to reap the benefits of what we sow. It is natural and healthy to be in that competitive state and important to us as it acts as a motivational factor to push us to do our best. But, I'm sure the stars in the sky don't compete with each other on whose light shines brighter. I'm sure the waves in the ocean are not haggling with each other or proving their levels of confidence based on their ability or speed to reach the shore. All I'm trying to explain to you is, it is **_Your Journey_**. Don't stop doing what you love. And it's ok if that day happened; it doesn't change the fact that you are blessed with divine talent, and you should spend your time discovering that part of you in all its glory, in its ups and downs. How would you feel, Alisha, if you saw me fail? Would you regret training under me? Would you respect me less? I'm sure you would not think along those lines; you would probably be my most encouraging student. Use some of your kindness towards yourself.'

Alisha was deeply touched by his words. Never before had they had such a profound conversation. She could see in his eyes the wisdom of ages and felt glad to be able to help herself from his vision and his experiences.

'Thank you, Anthony Sir, for your kind words and your time,' her eyes were full of tears. 'It means a lot to me.'

'Come, come now. Let us start practice. There are so many contests lined up, if you are interested.'

'Maybe in time, I will, Sir. For now, I will train.'

They began their practice, and it was a few days until she realised once again that this was indeed her safe space, something that she would never want to separate herself from again.

Chapter 5

She dialled his number late that night. Aarav picked up the phone in the first ring. 'Hey,' she whispered. 'Can I talk to Dev?'

A stab of jealousy passed through him for the first time. He was just leaving for Akshay's hostel. It was a twenty-minute drive if he took the road from behind his house. The male and female quarters were obviously separate, but groups of friends often made friends with the guards and got their way to hang out together until the wee hours of the morning.

'Yeah, sweetheart. Let me pass on the phone, hold on….'

Aarav & Alisha had spent the day together having lunch and a long talk near the lakeside. After that, they strolled along the Mall Road. They met their friends, and it was late evening when they went home. She never discussed anything about Dev with him, which made him relieved but uncomfortably curious at the same time. In the sense that they were really close now, he knew about all her friendships, her equation with her parents, cousins, all of it, but not with his brother. Nor did he understand how to ask about it; he was afraid they may be closer than he would be comfortable with. At that moment, he did not know how he would ask Dev what this call was about. It was a strange, insecure kind of feeling, which quickly disappeared when he was with Akshay, drinking whisky on the rocks along with smoking up all sorts of substances. This charade would not last too long…

'Hi, Alisha,' he sounded stiff on the line.

It pinched her insides. He would always call her Al. With time, it became increasingly evident that after she and his brother got close, these 2 indefinitely drifted far apart.

'Hi, Dev. It's been so long. How are you?'

'I'm good, been busy. Just got done with the medical entrance and placements will happen soon. How are you doing? What's up?'

'I'm fine. I wanted to catch up with you. How did the exams go, and when will the placement results be out? Feels like ages since we hung out. Let's meet tomorrow? Blue bench?' she asked hopefully.

'This week I'm really held up. I'll call you after that and surely let's meet. It has been a really long time.' He did not want to meet her; he felt weak in his knees and had the desire to confess things that he was forced to keep inside him.

She sounded rather disappointed.

'Well, alright. Do that. Also, I wanted to thank you for the doctors' recommendation. It went well. I will probably tell you more once we meet. And no, Aarav doesn't know yet. I plan on telling him in a couple of days. I also resumed vocal training, thought I'll share it with you….'

'That's awesome! Don't give up on that ever! Your voice will reach far. Take care, Al. I will see you soon.'

Alisha felt the warmth in that last sentence. How she missed him, talking to him, spending endless time with him. The biggest realisation that had hit her the most was that some relationship changes can be so subtle, yet so strong. *The same person is next to you, but you can't share the same equation with them because of circumstances.* How weird that felt. Like if she missed him, he lived close by. She could talk to him, but everything was different about the way they spoke, even though nothing was tangible. And from where he looked at it, he was suffering something that was the most beautiful part of his life.

When that bliss turned into his nightmare, was something he could not figure out. He longed to suddenly hold her, caress her, and be with her in a way which he never thought of before. Suddenly, his brother felt like the biggest threat to him, and he just wanted to go further and further away from the 2 of them. Mixed feelings of guilt and desire were incredibly hard to deal with, and he was beating himself over it time and time again.

'People choose their suffering, you know,' Naina said as they sipped on their tea the next evening.

'I never understand what you're trying to explain of late Naina.'

'That's because you are so preoccupied and stuck in your own assumptions since a while now.'

'Aren't we all?'

'Not really,' she said. 'Dev, it is only the ability to take perspective that may free you from feeling dejected. When you get to that level, you understand that every emotion of yours, if based on another person's decisions, will lead you to feeling ecstatic or disappointed on the basis of your expectations! And, when you are able to see that how things turn out is not only because of you, that everyone involved has their own story in it, it will lighten your burden.

'Have you ever pictured a scenario wherein, what if Alisha was waiting for you to come forward, and since it never struck you, in the meanwhile, Aarav showed interest, she probably just understood this as 2 different kinds of love? In your reality, you are feeling rejected. But in a whole new perspective, she hasn't even known anything about what you feel for her to reject you. Think about it.

'In her reality, she is probably wondering that you never thought of her as more than a friend. There are many such instances, even in friendships, familial equations, and so on. There is never a way to know why someone did what they did unless you are lucky enough to be that close to them, that you share their feelings with them and vice versa, provided they are at that wavelength. For you, it has become unrequited love, but for her, she may be just wondering why her best friend is so distant from her.'

He stayed quiet and deliberated for a long time. In the distance, the golden sun was dipping into the mountain gap, merging itself into the beautifully hued sky. Winter would soon begin, and the snowfall would cascade over the landscapes of the wonderful city.

'I need to move on, Naina. If I keep thinking of her, I will not be able to study. Thank you for always being there. You know, to listen to me rant about it over and over again. With your support and understanding, I will hopefully find my way out of this.'

'Try not to be too harsh on yourself. And stop being so formal and thanking me like we're in the middle of a seminar. Lighten up… and remember, you also have invested deeply in this friendship. Maybe it will make you feel better if you just stay in touch with her. It may hurt, yes… but it will probably hurt less than completely shutting yourself out.' Naina put her hand over his and squeezed it with reassurance.

Chapter 6

Aarav was holding up the string lights, and he was quite impressed with himself and the efforts he had put in. The hall looked beautiful with multi-coloured metallic balloons. Pretty flowers were interspersed with the balloon arrangement, with fairy lights everywhere! He had personally looked into the food menu, putting in some of her favourites, along with a lovely pastel floral buttercream cake. He had planned to take her shopping for a dress. His brother had refused to have anything done for his birthday when Aarav had suggested combining it. So he went ahead and planned it for her. She would be so happy, he thought!

He had curated the entire event on the terrace of her apartment. That way, it would be convenient for her parents to be a part of it. He also bought a neck piece for her in silver with raw-cut rubies, he would wear it on for her in the car he thought. He wasn't usually a sappy boyfriend, but with her, he kept redefining and reinventing himself. She was his partner, his friend, his lover, his companion. *But he still had to come clean about something. He was very hesitant to bring it up, with Dev's warnings ringing in his ears.*

He mentioned to all her friends and family to come to the lawn by 7 pm. And he had planned a few things with each one of them. He would enter with her at 7:30 as a surprise. He had completely distracted her. After he finished setting up, he left the odds and ends to the others. He then asked her to meet him in a new boutique which had opened so that he could buy her a birthday dress. When she finally liked one, he told her not to take it off; he wanted to take her out to dinner, he said. 'But Aarav, I haven't even told my folks I'm stepping out, let me go home and get ready. They probably want to have dinner with me,' to which he replied, 'Ok, but wear this, let's not waste time…I'll self-invite myself if you guys have plans!'

He had bought a car a few weeks ago, and their dreamy outings had increased with the privacy and independence. When they got into the car, he wanted to drive her home as a surprise. He held her hand softly before beginning to drive… 'I love you… happy birthday,' he whispered. 'I love you too…'

'Listen, there is something I want to tell you,' she hastily tried to bring it up.

Aarav glanced at his watch; it was 7:10. They had to be at her apartment soon.

'Tell me, all okay?'

'Well, it wasn't, but it is okay now.'

'What is going on?' he asked, worriedly.

'Look, I know you may wonder why I'm bringing this up now. But I wanted to be sure before telling you. The thing is, I… I… I visited a psychiatrist.' She felt silly. Why was she nervous and doubting herself?

So, what if she met a professional? If she was afraid of being judged by someone she loved, then was that even love? She never felt this way while telling her parents… Dev…she was confused.

He had no idea what she was talking about and what was going to follow. He stared at her blankly.

'Aarav, it's been a couple of years since I have been feeling out of sorts very often. But I could not put a finger on it, or understand it, or decipher it. And after the incident at the competition, it became increasingly difficult for me to find my self-confidence back. Stuff happened. I know I should have told you, but I was having panic attacks. You're my first… well… love or boyfriend or whatever you call it, and I was afraid to share it with you. I was scared of being judged, but I'm on mild medication, and my doctor says it is nothing to worry about, it is how you treat a physical ailment, and he is sure I'll get out of it. And I feel so much better now. The panic attacks were very difficult to cope with… so I finally decided to seek help. It's a case of acute anxiety.'

Aarav was quiet for a long time. She tapped him on his shoulder. He finally spoke, sounding hurt.

'So much is going on, and you never mentioned any of it to me? How is that even possible? Does Dev know?'

That was the question she was totally dreading.

'Yes, my family asked him for help. He got the doctor's contact from Naina. Please, let it just stay between us.'

'Stay between us? Wow. This is crazy. So you're dating me, and my brother knows the struggles in your life? And then after you have told him, you're telling me to keep it between us? What the hell is even going on? I get the good part, he gets the deep struggles part? What the hell?' He was fuming, his hands clenching the steering wheel.

'Look, Aarav. I didn't ask Dev, my folks did. We have been buddies since childhood and they wanted him to ask a known source for a contact, which wouldn't make things obvious and hard for me. Society is not forgiving, and my parents are not aware of these kinds of issues. For me, I don't care, but they don't have that cool awareness, and I cannot be spending my time convincing them that it's not taboo to talk about it. I can't force them to change their thinking overnight. I'm just glad I have supportive parents. The kind of stigma attached to having mental health issues is ridiculous. I'm sure you can be more supportive, right?'

'If you say you love me and you were going through something so big, I ought to have been the first one to know. Not after you have already gone to see a specialist.'

'Look, this is my first relationship. I was apprehensive and scared you might like me less. I know it sounds stupid but it takes time to confide in big things, right?'

Aarav suddenly felt a huge wave of guilt wash over him. This was not the way he wanted things to unfold, and he had not told Alisha anything about his alcohol and tobacco addiction, if he could call it that. She was right, it did take time to confide in big things. She knew Akshay as someone from college; she didn't know about the hostel, the nights, and the craziness. He drove in silence to her apartment. He wished she never said any of this to him . His brother's words were ringing in his ears. God, this was difficult.

As they reached her apartment, he parked his car, and they got out. No one spoke. He started walking towards the lawn, and she was confused. 'I need to go upstairs. Give me some time; I'll just come back…'

'Listen, don't be crazy… just please come here for a minute,' he said. He walked her towards the lawn, and soon the distant brightness was closer. In minutes, she saw that all the people she knew were in front of her.

Chapter 7

Alisha was pleasantly surprised to see so many people. It was a beautiful setting with flowers, fairy lights, and balloons. Everyone came close to wish her and greet her, and she was truly touched by his gesture. It was all smiles everywhere; she looked gorgeous in a white one-piece with her hair let down and a delicate pearl adorning her neck. Simple, elegant, and poised. Her eyes were scanning the crowd to make eye contact with him after their intense conversation in the car, when she locked glances with Dev instead. It had been a while. He looked so handsome in a white shirt and blue jeans; he tried to steer away, but it was too obvious, so he walked up to her. She suddenly felt guilty to talk to him, now that Aarav knew about her situation.

'Happy Birthday, Al,' he warmly hugged her.

'Thank you! Gosh, it's been so long. It seems like a different lifetime; we would hang out all the time.'

'Yeah, well. Things change. Anyway, how are you? You look great!' he tried his best to sound platonic.

'I'm good. Listen, sorry to spring this on you, but I thought I better tell you before he does. I told him about the panic attacks, and he asked me if you knew. I was dreading the question, and I don't know where that even came from because we don't spend time like we used to, and Aru is aware of that. But when he asked me, I could not deny it either. He is quite upset, more about the fact that I've been feeling this way and he doesn't know, and to top it off, you knew but he didn't. I tried explaining the fact we have been friends since childhood, etc. I don't know what state of mind he is in. Also, the last few times you have mentioned something about the monastery. I feel so disconnected from you. What is actually happening? When can we spend time and talk, Dev? We never even go to the blue bench anymore…' she trailed off…

The speed at which she spoke, Dev was filled with a desire to hold her. He missed spending time with her, the enthusiasm of her words, and the spark of emotional involvement in her eyes. His life seemed rather drab without her constant company. Out of choice, out of sight, out of mind – that was his present reality.

'I'm sorry, Alisha,' he sounded fed up. 'I think it's time I also face reality. The truth is, ever since Aarav and you got together, it definitely changed the dynamic of friendship between us. It is not something to be expressed in words, but it happens as an undertone. And I guess I stepped back because you and I were very invested in each other, and that is obviously not something you would want to overlap, that too in your first relationship. And for me, it was a bit different because that person is my own brother, and it definitely felt awkward.

'Regarding Dorje Drak, well, it is a passing thought; sometimes I feel like it's my calling. I go visiting there often, sometimes alone and sometimes with Naina. I'll tell you more about it when something materialises in my head first.

I didn't mean to scare you that day, ha-ha. But I may just surprise you!

'And yeah, for sure, Aarav will be very upset about me recommending a psychiatrist for you. Firstly, he doesn't even get these things. Anyway, I will explain my version to him when he asks me directly, you don't worry. He will be upset, but in a few days, he will understand where each one of us is coming from.'

Alisha felt relieved and comforted hearing his insights, and the way he always broke down situations and explained it to her so well. But that lingering sadness of not sharing the same bond with him hurt her. She wondered how he dealt with it, but he was pretty wise like that; she kept telling herself.

She missed being close to him. She sometimes started regretting the fact that she and Aarav were together, simply because it altered everything with Dev, and she was too naïve to understand it earlier, but now she did. It was just impossible to be close to both of them. She even became conscious of the fact that on a subtle level they shared a love they could never express, never manifest, and never acknowledge. And there was no way they would ever know because neither of them understood the depth of their feelings at that tender age. She felt a vacuum in her heart even though she was with someone; it was rather weird.

The pandemonium in her mind always teased her because the other part of her was giddy with excitement on most days, discovering the passions and flames of love and tenderness.

Soft music played in the background, and everyone took turns to come and speak to her and wish her. Her friends socialised with her family, and it felt complete to have all the people she cared about in one place. It was truly a special evening. She looked around with searching eyes for Aarav, who didn't seem to be around since they entered, after their argument. After a few minutes, she spotted him coming in from the back end of the lawn. She walked up to him hurriedly; she wanted to apologise for earlier and thank him for the evening. Dev told her all about how long he had been planning this evening for her; she was feeling so loved and cared for. As she walked towards him, she got the faint aroma of alcohol, or was it something else? She had noticed it a couple of times but had never asked. Why would he never tell her, prior or post it? There was something strange going on.

'Hey, love!' he swooned. 'Come, it's time to cut the cake.'

He seemed to fumble slightly, and her senses immediately were on guard. His walk was wobbly, too. He made it pretty obvious by then. She decided not to discuss it at that point. They walked back into the party, and the reek of alcohol from him was more evident as they walked closer to each other. She called out to her parents to come over for her to cut the cake. Both their families were around her; Aarav's parents were very fond of Alisha, and it seemed like a matter of time before this friendship would turn into a deeper bond.

He was unusually talkative. It was a matter of minutes until all their friends understood he had a bit too much to drink, so they took him away from the elders at the party.

But where did he go to drink? Why doesn't he say anything to me about it? These questions kept circling her mind.

She was completely preoccupied, but she wasn't able to break away from anyone at that point. She decided she would definitely ask him all about it first thing the next morning.

Chapter 8

It was 9 am when Aarav opened his eyes. The morning rays were piercingly bright through the gaps in his curtains. The theme and aesthetic of his room was very different from the rest of the house. With dim lights and high walls, it was like a hippy bachelor pad. He reached out to his mobile and saw a flurry of text messages from Akshay, Alisha, and Rohan, his superior at work.

A couple of months ago, getting access to a mobile phone seemed exciting, but he was already fed up with it. It seemed like people shed their reservations and spoke easily over text, whereas face-to-face, the talk was more real but reserved.

He was very disturbed when he read Alisha's texts. *'Are you okay, love?*

You reeked of alcohol last evening.

Don't you think it's something we need to discuss?

I know here and there you drink, I mean you have never mentioned but now I'm putting it together. But last night was scary; you were stumbling, it was sort of obvious. Mum and dad also asked me if you're okay.'

It beeped again in a few seconds.

'You made it such a big deal when I told you about my situation, and you're conveniently hiding this from me?'

His mind was reeling; didn't she have a good time at the party at all? He didn't expect this confrontation. He was expecting a *thank you for the lovely evening* kind of a conversation.

Rohan had asked for some documents that he had yet to assemble. He had misplaced some of the documents. He was a mess.

Akshay had messaged him regarding some new stuff. *'Waiting for you tonight, bro,'* it said. His heart began to race, his head was spinning with the hangover.

His phone beeped again; it was her again.

'Stop pursuing something useless, Aru. It's going to lead you to nothing.'

He was boiling with anger. How could she bombard him with messages like that? But, she did have a right to be angry. If he wanted to be such a deep part of her life, what was he trying to do? Was he angry at himself? He didn't react at that moment; luckily, they weren't face-to-face yet.

Minutes later, she called him.

'Hey! Morning!' she whispered. It sounded like she was yelling on text message. *Very misleading,* he pondered...

'Hey, hi. Good morning. What's up?'

'Well, what's happening? Why don't you tell me? Let's get to the point, no? You've been drinking excessively and haven't thought it important to tell me? I'm not saying it's a good or bad thing; I mean it's obviously not a good thing. It's just that you know my family and I don't drink or smoke, so I'm obviously apprehensive about these habits. And it felt really weird because you didn't even talk to me about it. What is this relationship based on? I have a huge problem because I know your routine from morning to night, and this doesn't make sense because you have never spoken about this. Like when do you go drinking? That means there are a lot of lies underneath this, right? Like I'm not okay with this much. A little here and there for fun is totally fine but this was scary. And to put 2 and 2 together, I'm trying to recall the last few times we've hung out; there has been some incoherence. Like I'm fixing the puzzle pieces now, and I notice your talk is different in the mornings and different in the nights, don't you notice it?' she went on and on until he interrupted her.

'Alisha, please, just take a breath!' he stuttered.

'Did... did last night mean nothing to you? The entire evening, the set-up. I've spent a month curating this night for you, and you just call me the next day and barrage me like this?'

They were both quiet for a while. He was so embarrassed by the way he was spoken to.

'I'm sorry. I had the best time; it was magical. It was so, so sweet of you to even think of something so grand. The gesture really touched me. It's just that, minutes prior to it, we broke into an argument, and throughout the night, I kept feeling bad for hiding all of it from you, when the truth is it was not an intentional thing to keep it from you. I was still figuring out a comfort zone, if I may call it that. Besides when you brought Dev's name into the conversation, it hurt more because we used to be close for almost all our growing up years. I'd like to think we still are, even though the equation between us is so different. And then you made me feel bad for taking his recommendation when you know we are… were…best friends. Who else would I trust? And to top it off, I had been in doubt that you are drinking something or smoking up something. I just never had the guts to ask. And last night, it just confirmed it for me when you almost slipped while coming close to me, and I could smell it. I was overwhelmed with anger that you are hiding it from me. And I just can't figure out at what time you do all this? Is it during the day or night or what? And then you're pointing a finger at me. Nothing makes sense; I didn't like it at all….'

'I'm sorry. I should have been more upfront,' he said. 'I think in my mind I have this double standard because alcohol and cigarettes are something people do, but medication is a huge deal. It was wrong of me. I apologise.'

'No, but you tell me something. When we plan to meet somewhere, do you drink at home and then come, or do you meet me and then go somewhere? Like, when do you do it? Because you keep saying you're stepping out with mum, or you're at the office, or you're going out for lunch/dinner, whatever, so is it during all of this?'

He didn't know what to say. She was quite a detective. He was quiet on the other line, which he knew would agitate her more, but he didn't want to argue on the phone.

'Aarav, let's meet and talk. Okay?'

'Yeah, at 5 pm. Wood Street Café?'

'Make it 7, please. Let's do dinner. I have training at the studio.'

'Ok.'

The air was nippy when Aarav stepped onto his balcony to smoke. Dev knocked on the door.

'I'll be shifting to the hostel soon. Three years for the biochemistry degree. My accommodation got confirmed as well.'

Aarav puffed away. 'Good luck and congratulations, that's such great news.'

Chapter 9

Wood Street Café was a small and charming cafeteria in the heart of the city. People often came there and sat for long hours, the ambience was such. Cosy, rustic, and comforting, legend had it that it was the café of good luck; once a wish was made and pasted on the walls there, it would come true! The wooden walls were all decorated with papers, and on the papers were people's wishes, desires, notes, thoughts, and so on. It was vibrant with young energy, and the ambience had quite the feel-good factor.

Alisha had dressed in a subtle sky-blue dress with her hair tied in a high ponytail when Aarav walked in. He was a bit tired from the previous night, his eyes could tell.

She had ordered his usual stroganoff and black coffee, and a lemonade with a croissant salad for herself. She wanted to come straight to the point, but her therapist had told her to observe the other person's mood or state of mind before initiating something important, or something that was going to impact the other person's thought process too suddenly. *'Give them time to process, and you take some time to process too,'* he had said. It was indeed an arduous 'process', constantly thinking, planning, and waiting to approach someone.

Luckily, he himself brought it up instantly. 'Look, sweetheart, I should have told you, but as you said, I know you are conservative in your thoughts about these things. I guess I did not want to freak you out, but obviously lying is not the way to do it.'

'Aru, I can understand other's needs. But some of this is definitely beyond me. Like, I don't have a problem with you drinking alcohol occasionally; maybe I would want to try it sometime too. But the fact that you kept it away from me makes me wonder, why would you not tell me? It's just that I don't even know when you fit it into your day. If you are addicted, then this is a challenge. Now, if I look back and try to put things together in my mind, I feel like you're in 2 different moods at 2 different times of the day. And smoking is hazardous; I feel like you hide it because you yourself are unsure of what you're doing.'

She paused but had to ask... 'We speak so many times in the day, you never mention that you're drinking or smoking, but when we meet, now that I think about it, you sometimes seem like you're saying stuff, but in the next moment there's no connection to what you said before... and if you're not bringing it up when we speak multiple times, are you saying goodnight and meeting someone?' Her heart was racing, and she could feel the panic. She regretted being so blatant. She wasn't sure if she wanted to hear his answers.

'I haven't thought about it like that. It started before I began work, with Akshay from college. You know him. Initially, it was occasional, but yeah, now I guess it is a bit much. We meet in the nights and jam with some good music, order food, and just chill, nothing else.'

'So, you never told me you meet him at night…? When we say goodnight, I assume we both are sleeping.

'I don't know what to say. I'm finding it a bit stupid. Like, for example, would you be in the same romantic mood if it wasn't you reacting in that moment of intoxication? Or how deep is this relationship? How intense would our conversations be if you were to be sober? It feels like what you're doing is shaping 2 different people inside you, and I don't know who I am with. And it's funny because we have been dating for almost 2 years now. How long has it been since you have been up to all of this?'

'Listen, Dev has been talking to you about all this?' Aarav blurted out.

'**What**? Dev knows?' She looked furious. Her cheeks were flushed.

Aarav looked downward. This was such a mess.

'Ok, look, now that we are talking about it, there is no use lying. Yes, he knows. And yes, he has warned me, and he wanted to tell you, but he obviously didn't because he gave our relationship respect and time to figure it out ourselves. And it started around… when I finished twelfth… it has been a while since I have been drinking and smoking. But earlier it was nothing, over the last few months, I think it has increased.' However bad it sounded, he was kind of relieved to say it aloud.

'You have **some** nerve then, to judge me and wonder why I kept my situation private. I told you in the first month of starting off with medication, I went through such hell feeling these panic attacks. And that is not even altering me as a person; it is just my journey making sense of my irrationalities. And then you got all upset that Dev knew. It's all so stupid. You expected me to trust you in a month when you kept it from me for so long? So basically our relationship doesn't exist, right? It is a reflection of your intoxication, and when you're sober, it is your mere habit. Am I right?'

Aarav felt like he had been slapped. He was very uncomfortable with the way he was being questioned, but he also understood her pain and resentment. He loved her deeply and it made him sick that she doubted that.

Brushing away the tears in her eyes, she stared into the distance for a few minutes. She wanted to get up and leave the place, but she didn't. He put his hand on hers and squeezed it.

'I love you, Alisha. I have made some wrong choices, but I love you. I'm crazy about you, and you are the only one I have felt this way for. Give me some time. I don't want to lie, but I'll try to cut down and structure myself.'

'Maybe, if you had made me a part of your experience, I would have known your state of mind. It just feels like our intimacy is driven by your intoxication, and that thought is bothering me. Like maybe if you're sober, you won't feel the same way about this relationship. That means…every time we have touched…it's such a creepy feeling now.' She cringed in a way that was making him angry, but he could not deny the truth of it.

'Think about it… Aarav, if we had to be just friends or didn't commit ourselves to each other, I would have been so supportive. But this label that 2 people give their relationship means it is heading somewhere. And when we are thinking of our future together, then it signifies putting our best foot forward so that we can be there for each other and deliver. We have to bring the best to the table. That's the difference between friendships and relationships in the world, and I do not judge you as a friend. But if we have to move forward, I know that all of these things will come in the way.'

Deep inside, Alisha felt this was the truth, and she was scared he would agree with it. It felt safer living in the bubble of non-confrontation, but she was bold enough to step up and discuss it.

'It is nothing like that. It's just that I have been too habituated, and I'm consuming more than required. I'm sure it is a matter of time until I just cut back and focus on other things. The way you're reading into it, making it sound like I'm intentionally trying to hurt you, that is not true. I agree it's not conducive to lie, but there is no hidden agenda, and all that about my feelings towards you… I love you to bits, and you know that. I'm not a mad person.'

They were quiet for some time, seemingly saturated with the conversation. She was so irritated and shocked that Dev didn't give her the truth. They were friends since childhood; how could he not tell her such an important aspect of his brother? But maybe she just answered her own question. How would he tell her about Aarav? He was obviously torn between the 2 of them. But that was still unfair, he should have saved the day by speaking the truth. But was it his place to talk? It was a hopeless situation wherein right and wrong seemed to merge, making things all the more problematic.

Taking Dr Amar's advice, she decided not to ask Dev anything about it until she processed what was happening. He surely has his reasons.

'I am taking part in a singing competition again. It is a small event, an inter-college cultural, but it's a duet this time. I'm kind of excited, but obviously overthinking it, as usual,' Alisha broke the silence.

'Oh my, that is the best news of the day. Nothing could make me happier,' he flashed his genuine big smile, and she felt in that moment that nothing was wrong. They sank into a feeling of ease.

Maybe things would get better in time.

Chapter 10

'So, why don't we explore when and how it began?' Dr Amar asked Alisha gently.

'It's been years now, doctor. It has intensified over the last couple of years, like I feel it more. But if I look at it closely, I may have never acknowledged it the way I do now. Although it definitely has been a part of my personality since early adolescence.'

'Well, that is good awareness. Tell me more.'

'Now, when I look back, I feel like it always lingered with me. Be it a birthday party or a family function, even when I was by myself, or sometimes at school; like a persistent sting that reminds you to be scared even when you're not. It gradually built into a sort of restlessness. I was very easily distracted, and trying to put my focus on something was a very demanding task. As I've grown older, it seems like it has intensified. And now I feel like a fish out of water every time I'm having a panic attack. The last year was terrible with it being continuous. Now, after you have put me on the muscle relaxant, it feels like a weight has been lifted off my shoulders. It is like I can see the feeling from a bit of a distance.

'I had a lot of trouble concentrating on things, even basic tasks like bathing, brushing my teeth, and getting ready. Getting ready to go out was the worst; I would feel like I'm stuck in a whirlwind which I could not get off, and it would lead to my head throbbing. I could never sit down to eat a meal; I had to eat everything while standing or doing something else. I didn't realise this was a problem, but it was such a habitual part of my routine. Maybe I should be thankful for that competition when my voice refused to come out. From the outside, it probably looked like I failed at something, but really it was the birth of my clarity about this condition I have been going through.'

She was glad to be able to speak about her experience in such a cohesive manner.

'So, what the muscle relaxant does is, it numbs the feeling. Like I explained, it doesn't cure the anxiety, but it can suppress it to give you momentary relief. The need for this will be based on the underlying cause of why you have the anxiety. If it is physiological and genetic, let us assume, you can slowly find alternate therapies and exercises to help you balance it. If it is psychological, we can work side by side with a counsellor who will shed light on the reasons behind these feelings.'

'Is it a problem, doctor, if I continue with the medication?'

Alisha was surprised at her own question. From someone so reluctant to even visit the practitioner, she felt so secure with taking the medication that she now worried how she would feel without it.

'No, there is no problem. But if it can be resolved with counselling, I don't see a need for continuing it beyond a certain point. But anyway, we will cross that bridge when it comes.'

'Is there anything else you would like to share?' he suggested. 'The more input I have, the more I can try to help.'

'I feel awkward sharing this experience. Not many people understand, and I feel people will think I'm crazy or something.'

'Well, yes, people don't make it easy. But that is when we need to get stronger. When the body is haywire, no one calls it crazy. What people are unable to comprehend is that physical and mental ailments are deeply connected. Everything in the body is connected, and it is a reflection of the state of mind. But there is no possibility of explaining such details to anybody. These are changes that happen over spans of years. *There is nothing wrong in feeling what you are feeling.* And there is nothing wrong in keeping it private. In fact, the more people you tell, the more unnecessary opinions, suggestions, and interactions will be at your front. It is advisable to keep it to your close-knit circle. Not everyone is blessed with the capacity of understanding and empathising.'

He altered the dose of her medication to see how she responds and scheduled her next visit after 2 months, to be interspersed with counselling sessions once every 3 weeks.

As she was exiting, she bumped into Naina.

'Hey! What a nice surprise...' she smiled.

'Hi, Naina! Indeed, Dev mentioned to me that you're doing your internship here. Thank you so much for the reference. It's been so helpful.'

'You're most welcome. I hope you're feeling better. Dr Amar is really on point.'

'Well, yes, I'm definitely feeling better. I should have called and thanked you personally. I'm sorry. It was a bit difficult for me initially.'

'No, not at all. I understand. I've been working part-time here for 6 months. I have to submit my PhD thesis next year, and Dr Amar runs the training programme for us. It's amazing to train under him. He has insights that are pretty simple yet ground-breaking, if you ask me. Like he will say it in a way that makes you wonder how you missed it. I find it amazing!'

'Undoubtedly... let's catch up when you're free! How about Sunday evening?'

'Yeah, let's do that!'

It was 2 o'clock in the afternoon, and Alisha had to be at the training centre at 4 o'clock. She went home, had lunch, updated her mum about her visit, and then took a walk to the training studio.

She had resumed training some time back. It felt great, but sometimes memories of that evening made her confidence waver. This time she chose to train in a group; she felt safer, and it was really nice because she met some new people and they formed a nice group of friends amongst themselves. She was performing a duet with her classmate Sanjay, and they were yet to decide on a song with Anthony Sir.

It was a long day, and Alisha lay in bed waiting for Aarav to call at his usual time. It was past 10 pm, and when she called him, there wasn't an answer. She called Akshay worriedly; he didn't answer either. A minute later, he called her back, with the familiar slur in his voice that she now knew unmistakably. *Unbelievable, just unbelievable. After all we discussed*! She tossed and turned but wasn't able to go to bed. She tried calling Dev; maybe he would somehow bring up the topic and tell her what he knew as well. Dev saw her number flashing on the screen but didn't answer; he knew it would be about Aarav. He was dreading the day she found out about all of this, mostly about the fact that he knew and obviously didn't tell her.

Chapter 11

What comes to you, comes for you.

'Let's do the song 'Love Story', the old song. We could do a duet on it,' Sanjay suggested.

'Yeah, it's a superb tune to play on the piano. It's by Andy something, no?' Alisha replied.

'It's called *Where Do I Begin?*' by Andy Williams.

'I forgot. Let's try it out.'

'But, it is tough, the tenor has to dip very low.'

'It's okay, let's try. If we're not in sync, we will think of something else.'

'But the vocals are few in this. Does it make sense doing it as a duet...?'

'Tell me some other options also? Dancing in the dark is nice, by Bruce Springsteen... we could add our own twist to it, obviously, to make it a duet...'

They were pondering when he noticed the light on her phone constantly flashing.

'Hey, your phone is beeping.'

'It's ok.' She silenced the phone and looked at Sanjay.

She was beginning to avoid Aarav's calls since the last call. It really triggered her anxiety now that she identified him as sober and as an alcoholic, and she had a strong feeling he was doing something during the day too. It made her struggle with her expression of emotions. Her problem was she felt he was lying, which was a bigger issue than what he was doing.

'Hey, are you okay? You look unwell.'

Alisha didn't realise. She looked like she was getting blurry-eyed. She felt incoherent; her body shivered, and she looked left and right, feeling helpless. It was so embarrassing to keep going through this. Sanjay brought her a chair and some water. She sat down for some time, shaky and dizzy, his hands were on her shoulders. It took a few long moments for her to regain self-control. Just a few moments later, the housekeeping lady, the caretaker of the centre, came in and informed her that someone was waiting for her outside, in the portico.

Sanjay held her hand and led her out. She wasn't expecting to see anyone, and in that zone, she walked along with him. She saw Aarav and Dev standing together and was beginning to think she was delirious. Sanjay slowly let go of her hand and started to walk back inside without saying anything.

Aarav was about to speak when he noticed she was not in her element. She was confused at seeing the 2 of them together.

'Are you okay, Al?' Dev came close to her.

'Yeah, I just wasn't feeling up to it. Having a tough rehearsal. What's up? How come you *both* are here? What's going on?'

'I wanted to tell you that I'm leaving for the hostel tomorrow. I wanted to say bye. It's a couple of hours drive, but I'll try to visit often! Aarav wanted to have a chat with you, apparently, so he said he'll come along with me.'

None of them spoke; they just stared at each other. At that point, Dev felt it was his cue to leave. He leaned in and hugged Alisha.

'Why are you so low Al, your eyes are all blurry. Are you not feeling better with the meds? What is happening?' He was concerned about her, she seemed like she was struggling.

'Nothing that I can discuss right now,' she sounded drained out.

'Call me when you can.' He left, half smiling.

It was still the most painful emotion he was feeling, forcing himself to be away from her. Always reminded of the fact that had he just known he was so deeply in love, he would have told her, and none of this would be his reality. He wanted to take her in his arms and comfort her anxiety, but he couldn't even talk to her the way he used to anymore.

He sighed and went along. He didn't expect a response from Alisha, what with Aarav standing right there. And he knew they had so much to sort out between themselves. He knew she was upset with him for not telling her the truth about him too, but there was little he could do. He thought of telling her some time back, but he didn't have the heart to do that to Aarav. He had even asked Naina what to do, but for the first time, she too was confused. It was a rather delicate dilemma. There were chances he could have created more damage, what if Aarav denied it… so many possibilities. Better not to interfere since they are romantically involved, he had finally decided and left it at that.

'Why are you avoiding my calls, Alisha?' Aarav asked, oblivious to her irritation.

'Are you crazy or something?' she snapped.

'You're not even answering my calls at night, and you're asking me this in the morning? You're living in your own world. You are aware that I was trying to reach out to you last night? You were slurring. Who do I speak to? I feel like I'm in a relationship with your bottle or your cigarette, not you! I think it is better we take a break.'

Aarav felt like he had been punched in the gut. He was confused and didn't believe she was trying to end things.

'C'mon, it's not that bad. I told you I will work on it, and we will figure this out together.'

'We can figure it out together if you communicate with me when you're sober. Barely 2 weeks ago, we spoke at the café, and you said you're going to work this out and stop lying, all of that rubbish. If you come up with a plan, then execute it too. Why don't you understand? You need to draw some boundaries and get disciplined. If you're going to do this every day, there is no relationship. I basically have no clue about your whereabouts. There is only your imagination of me. *It feels like 2 people living in the same mind; it scares me.'*

'Who was that boy holding your hand? Why was he holding your hand?'

'See what I mean? I was having a bloody panic attack. He was just concerned. He doesn't know me like you do. There isn't any trust, also, in this relationship. It's really saturating me, emotionally and mentally.'

'It's not that I don't trust you. I don't know him from Adam. Look at it from my point of view. I agree we have problems, but if you see me traipsing along holding a girl's hand, I don't think you would be comfortable.'

'Understandable, but don't justify your behaviour, your lies, your intoxication in unnecessary quantities. How are you ever going to be there for me, for us, if you don't even know what you're doing? You're asking me now why I'm not answering your calls. You're not understanding that you have done the same thing at night, is it? And what do you mean that we will figure it out together? I cannot even understand when all this is happening?'

Alisha continued, a lot more coherent and confident. Repeated explanations were just going to repeatedly trap them.

'Look, Aarav, a lot has changed for me after we started dating. First things first, I have never been in a relationship before or even flirted with a guy... I used to be really close with Dev, and when that friendship disappeared, it took a toll on me, but I do understand the dynamics. I also started prescribed medication, which is another leap for me. What I'm looking for right now is comfort and emotional security; I'm not looking for a roller coaster ride. So, if you can please understand, I feel it is better we step back for a while. Let's try and figure out who we are out of this equation, and let's talk more as friends so we understand each other's temperament. There is no point giving our relationship a tag, and then building expectations, and then watching all of it crash, when we can rather share a mature friendship on a deeper level.'

She gave his hand a gentle squeeze and started walking back to the studio.

Alisha didn't know if what she said to him was right or wrong, but she was exhausted with the pulse between them. If she couldn't feel safe in his company, something was surely amiss. She felt terribly lonely. Dev was leaving for the hostel. She broke up with Aarav.

But some part of her was intact. She was beginning to find herself outside of her relationships with people.

Chapter 12

How much darkness are you willing to go through, to finally become the light?

Dev was writing down some of his musings in his journal. His new accommodation in the hostel was peaceful. It was a dormitory with 4 hundred rooms in his premises split into 2 buildings. There were many medical student residents from all over the country. His room was not very spacious, but he kept it simple with a small study near the window and a one-door cabinet for his clothes. Dev believed in simple living, not keeping more than what was required, and that really helped him unclutter his mind. He was happy with his new piece of work and was trying to submit it to the college magazine.

Smoky winds engulf purple space,
Earth bounces in a liberating embrace,
Yellow leaves rest on the trees' entirety,
Rainbows know seven colors as one entity.
White torrents rupture, breaking indigo rime.
Life sips on existence, time to time,
Dual ends of grey linger, black and white,
Radiance in darkness is never seen in light.
Starts rupture, lonely amidst multitude,
No one holds a daring to delineate rectitude,
Black currents of fortune hurl boats of being,

Promises boomerang as errant doing.
Wisdom predicts destiny. Fear impedes sanctity.
Flakes of fire sedate a burn,
Dew sparkles, even on an ashen fern.
Marionette played by strings,
In a lavender wave, inaudibly sings,
In the Earth, bouncing to mesmerise,
I twirl in smoky winds, hypnotised.

He wrote the last line in his keepsake journal too and was looking for his phone. 'Hypnotise' was the title he gave the poem.

He had changed a lot over the last few months, but whatever changes he went through, one feeling refused to fade away: *the regret he felt for not telling Alisha his feelings at any given point in time.* That made him feel vulnerable. It was as if something kept tugging at him, following him like a shadow. Aarav had called him a few nights ago to tell him that she ended things, saying she wanted to take a break. He was breaking inside, but he thanked God he was far away from the city limits. He would not want to be around either of them at this point. It would be too much to deal with. Now was not the time to tell her about his feelings for sure. That would be selfish and make all 3 of them feel so awful. As usual, he decided to leave it to fate.

It was past 4 o'clock. Dev called Naina, wondering where she was. She said she would come there around half past 3. She wanted to visit him and spend some time, it had been a while. As he was dialling her number, his room phone rang. The warden mentioned he had a visitor, and they didn't allow visitors in the rooms. He took his journal and water bottle and headed down.

Naina waited in the reception in a pair of blue jeans and a beige kurta. She looked quite tired and had a bundle of books next to her. She smiled as she saw him approaching. They hugged each other and went to the garden for a walk, leaving their belongings at the reception.

'It is so good to see you, Dev. It's been so long. See how things change, before we could meet once a week, and now it's been 2 months already!'

'Seriously… it's been good though. The course is just what I wanted, the people are nice. I met a really sweet girl too. I think it may go somewhere, but I'm not sure yet.'

'Oh wow!' Naina swooned in excitement. 'Tell me more!'

'Nothing, nothing. It's in my head right now. She is 2 years senior to me, so she has only one year to go. We meet at the library and exchange notes and stuff. We hang out a lot after lectures and sit together to study… all of that. There's a lot of attraction, and we both feel it. Her name is Isha. But I'm not getting the feelings I have for Alisha, I mean obviously. Like that tenderness and vulnerability, I'm sure that comes with time.'

'If you meet her in the library to exchange notes, I'm afraid it isn't going anywhere,' she laughed.

'Ha-ha! Thanks, but I can't be bothered to invest my emotions. I have zero clarity, but it's just nice to have company around here, you know. It kind of gets monotonous with the crazy study schedules and all… you would know best.'

'Well, of course, but it's healthy to see you trying to move ahead… How is Alisha, though? Are you both in touch? In fact, I met her at the clinic the other day, and then she said we should catch up.'

Dev started walking out of the gate. He had to sign the register before exiting. There was a nice park close by, which they started walking towards.

'Aarav told me they are on a break.'

'What happened?'

'I don't know. It must be because of his habits, I feel.'

'How does that make you feel?'

'Regret. I didn't know I harboured such intense feelings for her until she started dating Aarav, right? It seems a bit of a dead end for me. I don't think I'll ever find anyone in my life and feel for anyone the way I felt with her, in terms of compatibility, being myself, in almost every aspect. And now that they are taking a break, I feel very tempted to tell her everything, but I know it would be so wrong of me, like I'm taking advantage of the situation. It is like I have a dark side! So that is definitely something I have to refrain from. At the same time, it's a huge block for me with Isha, like something is stopping me. I will not let anything get intense with anyone now, you know?'

He continued, 'I know you probably think I'm over-analysing…'

'No, I'm glad you are. People get in and out of relationships so easily, as if it is a one-day affair. Its better you analyse it and think things through, before you drop this baggage on your future relationships... unconscious baggage is inevitable. This awareness can at least help you navigate right?'

'Exactly... That's exactly what I was thinking too. No point in creating a mess when things are already unclear in my mind. Anyway, that is enough about me, what is up with you?'

'Things are good, really good. I'm working on my thesis. I'm so glad I decided to do my PhD. It's a lot of work, but I do feel I have breakthrough insights. I have been visiting the monastery as well, and a young apprentice who has joined their administration team is helping me with a lot of information. Getting to talk to the Samanera is not easy, but he said once or max twice, I may get an opportunity to share some insights and get productive feedback on what I'm doing and why, etc...

'Did you visit again? You were planning to, no? You were saying you wanted to tell me something... I'm unsure...'

He looked down at his shoes pensively. 'I did. It felt a bit foolish in retrospect, but at that point, I remember I was so restless.'

'You still haven't told me what happened that day. I've been waiting, but obviously, I understand if you are not comfortable talking about it...'

'No, I'm okay now. It was just a few days into my degree course, and I was a complete wreck. Since I had toyed with the idea of joining the monastery, I had convinced myself that it was my calling. But when I went there, things didn't unfold the way I thought they would...' He continued, 'I reached there in the wee hours of the morning and...' He went on to describe his experience.

Dev sat down in the shade of the big banyan tree. He had been waiting for more than an hour to meet His Holiness, Mr. Yansuk. He was the Head Administrative Monk, who would interview him on his reasons to join the order. Boys as young as 11 years old were already part of the monastic order, but they were always put through a series of questions and prerequisites before being allowed.

He spotted a middle-aged man clad in a deep maroon robe with orange borders on the edges, walking slowly towards him. The aura around him was exuding a calm exuberance, and Dev felt blessed and lucky to be able to share physical space with him. He bowed down in respect, and Mr. Yansuk nodded in reverence. He spoke matter-of-factly.

'Do you want to sit in the office or under this tree?'

'Wherever you say, Your Holiness.'

'Where do you want to sit?'

He felt a tinge of fear and apprehension.

'Here, under this tree'.

'Let us sit. Why, young boy, do you want to join us?'

'I feel very calm in the presence of this place. I feel it is my calling.'

'Then, you can visit anytime you like. Why do you want to be a part of the Order?'

He did not know what to say. He never did think this through.

'It has been a few years since I have been thinking of joining the Order. I feel safe in these surroundings.'

'What do you do?'

'I am studying, your Holiness. I have a degree in Biochemistry.'

'You have chosen to be a doctor to serve and help humanity, am I right?'

He kept quiet and nodded slowly.

'Tell me more about yourself.'

'I live at Clifton Apartments with my brother and parents.'

'No, son, tell me about you.'

'Well, I am a thinker. I love to draw. I love art, I love to write, and I love my family.'

'There, then, you have your answer.'

'Answer?, What question did I ask?'

'You did not. Your eyes ask. Your eyes are searching for meaning, and you think this is your calling. Maybe it is, but this is not the time for you to join the Order, son.'

Dev stared into the distance, not understanding what he meant, but he felt a painful relief. Did that mean some part of him was equally in doubt?

'Son, has someone sent you here?'

'No, Your Holiness. I have come here on my own. I have been visiting for a few years. Unrequited love made me realise this is my path.'

'Pain of any kind can be understood and empathized with, but this is not the reason one should commit to leaving their duties and responsibilities.'

'But of what use is my existence? I am sure I will find my purpose once I am granted the honour of joining the Monastic Order.'

'Purpose is never found by escaping one's duties. Purpose is never found by questioning one's existence. When you fell in love, did you question your existence? No, you did not. You began to question it once you realised that the love you expect to be returned to you is unrequited. That unreturned love cannot be a reason for you to join us, would it be fair to you or the Order? No. Those cannot be the basis.

His Holiness paused briefly, stared into his eyes, and continued.

'Look at the roots and branches of this tree, how many millions of years it has been standing strong right here. Look at the tiny flowers about to blossom on your left, and turn right and look at the dried leaves and flowers fallen on the floor. What would you answer if the tree asked you, 'Why do I need

to provide shade to you?' Does the tree have a choice of who takes shelter underneath its branches? Now, look up at the sky, look at the clouds floating by, and look at the gaps in between where there are no clouds. Tell me, if they had to fight, what would they fight for? Does nature question its existence? Will stars fight on whom to shine their light on more?'

Dev was bewildered. His eyes were brimming.

'Our purpose is to exist in our full capacity. The pain you are going through is a lesson to open doors to your purpose. Please do not lose hope, and please do not neglect the duties that you have towards your family, well-wishers, and your career. Stay in the protection of the Divine Light. Come here when you feel the need to refuel your soul. The doors of Dorje Drak will always welcome you.'

'With that, he joined his hands and walked away into the distance, and I was in tears as I turned around, back in the face of reality.'

Naina was fascinated by what she had just heard. So soulful, gentle, enlightening, and simple. The truth of life in a few words. She leaned in and gave him a long hug. It seemed too intense for his age, and she was wondering what his mind was made of. It was a lot to absorb.

'Anyway, that's in the past. Let's go, I'll show you around the hostel, and there's a pretty cool café. I'm sure you're hungry as always!'

'Yeah, I want to eat something first. Then you show me. It's a pretty cool place, isn't it? So huge. How is the library here? Is it okay if I check out some books too? I want to borrow a couple if it is allowed, as in if you can do it in your name. I'll return it in 3 weeks.'

'Yeah, I don't think that should be a problem. I need a coffee badly, been over studying. Hey, I'm submitting something in my college magazine. I'll share it with you… let me know if you can relate to it.'

They strolled around, and she left back to the city late that evening, hoping to meet in the next couple of weeks. She felt satisfied after spending the day with Dev. It was mainly with his support that she got through her hard times and managed to pick herself up from where she was a few years ago.

Chapter 13

Don't take from someone what they don't even have...

Aarav was distraught. It had been a little more than 4 months since Alisha had completely stopped talking to him. Even when he made the effort to go to the places where he knew he would find her, she would acknowledge him, sometimes talk out of sheer formality, and sometimes she would silently walk away. It was so awkward. Aarav was alien to himself. All this while, the kind of attention he got from people made him feel important, gave his life meaning, and gave his personality some depth. The rejection he faced from Alisha hurt his ego, but he didn't know the art of self-reflection. He didn't know what to make of this door closing in on him. It was also the first time he let someone into his world, and part of him felt betrayed even though he knew he should not have been lying to her when she was crystal clear with him about what she felt.

What added to the awkwardness was that they were family friends. So, both their parents didn't take their fights seriously, which annoyed them so much more.

Alisha, on the other hand, was coping well. She had her bouts of self-doubt, but she knew better than to let her emotions get the better of her. If Aarav really wanted her, he needed to be honest about things. They had to be in an arrangement that suited both of them, not just one of them. And what was the point of getting trapped in a spider's web?

She had grown as a person. Her counselling sessions had helped her draw necessary boundaries with people, helped her be assertive and vocal about her needs, and helped her accept that there was no need to shy away from the anxiety she had. *When you embrace it, it can be your motivating fuel to do bigger and better things with yourself. Easier said than done*, she thought while trying to repeat the doctor's words to herself, but she wasn't so keen on embracing it; she just felt okay letting it be there while going about her regular day. She tried to look at herself and what she was experiencing as 2 separate things, which often left her confused. *'You will eventually get there,'* he had said.

She really missed Dev. She wanted to ask his advice eagerly on how to cope, and, more than anything, she wanted their friendship back to how it was. She often wondered if she loved him, but the guilt would shroud every other emotion. There were times she would take his journal, which he left with her, to the blue bench, read his poems, look at his doodles, and be happy to feel his presence. What different kinds of love she felt.

She kept busy as her competition was due the following week. Sanjay and she were putting in hours of practice, and she was a lot less nervous than the first time she stood on stage. Having someone by her side calmed her nerves, and she was able to sing a lot more confidently. This time around, she didn't extend the invitation to the concert to anyone apart from her parents. Dev was anyway not in the city limits, and she hardly spoke to Aarav. She was feeling strange at how different things were this time around, and she felt a tug in her heart.

The day of the competition had come, and Anthony Sir had encouraged her a lot. He told her that it didn't matter what the outcome was; it was all a learning experience. Alisha shrugged. She knew that in her heart, winning and losing were not what bothered her. It was her own struggle, her own thought process, her nervousness that she wanted to conquer. But first, she had to accept that part of herself, everything else would follow, Dr Amar had said, whatever that meant. She was just grateful that she didn't have that itchy throat.

The competition had started, and Alisha's duet with Sanjay was only in the latter segment. They were all sitting in the dressing room chatting, rehearsing, and encouraging each other. Alisha felt the familiar tremors rise within, and she tried to dismiss it. After all, she was now on medication, and it was not going to be severe, she told herself. She felt the beads of sweat forming on her forehead, the familiar dizziness of the same situation last time. Sanjay immediately noticed that she was zoning out. She wasn't responding to a word he was saying. But he knew now, instead of panicking, he brought a cold towel and dabbed her forehead a few times. 'Take deep breaths, its ok if you don't want to do this. Don't worry, we will get another chance...' He was tensed; this was his big chance too, but he didn't want her to feel pressurised.

Alisha felt embarrassed, but she knew she couldn't let him down. He had been the most supportive friend in the last few months, and during training, they had gotten really close. She knew it meant a lot to Sanjay; his passion for singing was the same, and she didn't want to rain on his game.

For him, he had to fight his way to be here. Unlike hers, his family was agonizingly unsupportive. *'What a waste of all your time, in a stupid studio!'* Those were the kind of harsh comments he would hear, and she knew his struggle was on another level. She would definitely not let him down!

'I'm fine, Sanjay, thanks. The cold towel helps! Just the usual thought process, you know how hard it is to break free from the shackles of the mind. I'll be fine... let's practice it once more before heading up on stage. We've got this.'

Chapter 14

Do it for all those people who believed in you, even when you couldn't believe in yourself...

The emcee was an enthusiastic and fun guy. He was interactive with the audience and good at engaging the crowd, without being too pushy or loud. This competition was being conducted at the State Level, and he also mentioned that the 3 winners would go on to participate with national competitors in the next 6 months. Following this, those 3 winners at the nationals would be felicitated with an opportunity to record their own album (with mentors), and their music compositions would be aired on All India Radio.

The crowd had gathered, and Alisha's parents, along with Sanjay's family, sat together. He didn't expect any of them to turn up, but his sister had forced their parents to come. She was eager to change their mind set and told them that once they saw the grandeur, the arena, the number of participants, and most importantly what a respectable talent it was, they would definitely not have the heart to discourage him.

They were assigned front-row seats since their children were performing. It was different from the Voice of India competition, which was mellow and elegant. This one had a more fun vibe, with laser lights across the auditorium showcasing neon graffiti walls and placards decorating the arena. It was a themed competition called Love Above All, and the theme was music that expressed love in all forms.

The director of the show was giving out instructions to the participants, explaining the order of events to them. Alisha and Sanjay were going to perform fifth in line. It was decided in a specific order, and they had all practiced the cues which would lead to the next act. As they were dispersing into their own desks to get ready, Alisha went in to check her phone. Sanjay was in conversation with some fellow contestants, and she noticed his expression was rather miffed. She went in a bit closer while looking at her phone and overheard bits of their conversation that made her feel rather upset.

'Why is she so weird? She will ruin your chances, bro,' Ajay whispered a tad too loud.

'If she's always a wreck, why is she doing this?' Neha added her own input.

'Dude, she seems a bit off, like crazy...'

'Yes, she always looks so nervous, doesn't she?'

It went on, and Alisha was getting into a tizzy.

They were obviously referring to her.

Her heart was racing abnormally, and she could feel her need to scream, but she felt choked at the same time. Everything felt hazy.

'Mind your own business, guys. Stop judging people. Just because someone is going through stuff which you people cannot relate to, don't sit here and make comments. Sick!' Sanjay retorted and walked towards Alisha. She heard him, but what the others had said was playing frantically on her mind. He didn't know if she had heard anything at all. When he saw her, he calmly sat down and went through the paper where the cues for each act were printed and given to all the contestants.

'Let's practice one last time,' he smiled.

Chapter 15

Don't put yourself up by putting others down.

The crowd was cheering the contestants as they all came up on the stage. The first act was the best, with all the pairs of contestants doing a joint rendition of *Love Me Do* by the Beatles. What a lovely vibe it was! The sponsors had gone all out to ensure this competition had the works in terms of décor, lighting, sound, and it was open to the masses, unlike the previous one Alisha had participated in. A much, much bigger crowd, she noticed.

The show started, and there were some rather beautiful performances of old songs in new voices. The third performance fell short, with the contestants not being in sync with each other. Looking closely, it was Neha and Ajay, *instant karma*, one would think!

Alisha and Sanjay gave a smashing performance. She swallowed her nervousness and prayed hard not to let him down. The crowd was cheering loudly for them, and Alisha felt on top of the world. Tears of joy streamed down both their eyes backstage, and she profusely thanked Sanjay for being such a huge support system. This really helped boost her confidence, and she went to the area where the coaches of different academies were seated to meet Anthony Sir.

She was looking for him, but she couldn't see him and was ushered back to her desk.

She and Sanjay finally got some downtime to talk and were super relieved that months of training were now done, and they could take a breather. She openly asked him what those other contestants were saying, and he tried to dismiss the topic, but she was persistent. He couldn't be fake with her, even though he didn't want to hurt her feelings by repeating their nonsense.

'Leave it, Alisha. All these comments aren't worth talking about.'

'Tell me, I want to know. I know you think I'll feel bad. Obviously, I will. But it's not like you have said it. I just want to know…' she insisted.

'Hmm. They were just being mean and making comments…' He trailed off…

'Sanjay, I don't mean to make you uncomfortable. I just want to understand how I come across as a person. I know I seem different from others, probably not normal either.'

'That's why I didn't want to get into this topic. Because you will put yourself down. There is nothing wrong with you, and there is nothing wrong in being different either, if that is how you put it. In fact, according to me, you are brave. Even though you are going through so much, you still muster up the courage to put yourself out there, seek help, and follow your passion at a point where most people would be in denial. Being young, maturity comes to only a few.

'Come on, and just because mind struggles are not tangible to the eye, it doesn't mean they don't exist, right? It's just that with this stupid imaginary pressure that some so-called society has put on people, and the baggage carried forward by generations of literally the same crap, it has become out of bounds to talk about it. Personally, I find it strange to ridicule anybody. And it's sad because most of us are surrounded by immature people who are trying to validate their own insecurities through ridiculing others, who are trying to put themselves up by putting others down. So, I don't think you should pay attention to all this negativity. We all have our own journeys, better to concentrate on ourselves and spend time with those who get it, right?'

'Wow! I knew you understood me and are empathetic about what I am going through, but you've taken me by surprise. You have so much perception about this; it sounds like your story needs to be told. Care to share?'

Sanjay fell silent for a few moments.

'My dad,' he shrugged, 'struggled a lot... with... you know...but he doesn't get it, he feels it is taboo to discuss it, he doesn't acknowledge it, so he is unable to get out of it. And I feel that is why he gives me such a hard time too.'

The emcee rushed in and called them outside. It was time for the results. Enthusiasm and excitement filled the arena, the thrill was palpable. All the contestants had assembled on stage to hear the results and then for the closing act.

Chapter 16

Winning and losing are part of the game, but which part of the game teaches us the same?

The contestants waited with bated breath. The air was tense, and a slow instrumental song was playing in the background when the chief guest came up to the stage to say a few words and hand out the prizes. There were inspirational quotes, amusing anecdotes, and special mentions made.

'The third place goes to... Nikhil & Swati for their wonderful rendition of *Love is in the air.*'

The second place goes to 'Sanjay & Alisha.'

Alisha's ears began to ring loud. She couldn't hear the applause, and she couldn't hear the cheering voices. She completely blanked out and stared ahead when Sanjay nudged and gently pulled her up to the center of the stage. He was ecstatic. She was right in front now and saw her parents.

'Alishaaa... why aren't you excited?' Sanjay asked her animatedly.

'I... I... I am! Oh my God, did we actually win?'

'Hahaha.'

She broke into a wholesome smile and went ahead to congratulate the first prize winners who did a medley of a few famous songs. One of them was her good friend Anna's brother, Andrew, and his partner, Milan.

They received cash prizes and an automatic entry into the national levels of the singing competition, which was going to be held in another few months. As they had lined up with the chief guest and other dignitaries to take pictures, Alisha suddenly noticed Aarav standing a few rows behind her parents, clapping and cheering.

Her heart fluttered and sank at the same time. It had been a long, long time since they spoke to one another. Passing by here and there, she tried her best to stay away from him. But where would the feelings hide? She knew she would have to face them someday, accompanied by the undeniable remorse of putting her friendship with Dev at stake. It was just a crazy rollercoaster ride.

Chapter 17

Some parts of you will change, and some parts of you will not change, and that is absolutely okay.

They sat at their regular seats at what used to be their favourite – the Wood Street Café. A strange silence brewed for a while, but neither of them felt uncomfortable. Meeting at some point was rather predictable, but what was going to be the outcome?

'Alisha, I haven't been drinking as much. I restrict myself to weekends,' he came straight to the point.

'How are your parents? How is Dev?' she said with an ache in her heart.

'All good. How are things at your end?' he felt rather dismissed.

'Going on.'

'I'm so thrilled that you're going to be participating in the nationals! So proud of you, always knew you would make it.'

'Thanks,' she smiled. 'Although it's more an inner vibe, which I'm rather grateful for. I feel so much better now. It is a lot of effort to work on oneself,' she continued. 'How is work going along, better now?'

His face fell. He didn't know how to tell her that he was fired. It was embarrassing, but he decided to speak the truth instead of again spiralling in a mesh of lies and ruining his remote chance of being a part of her life again. Aarav, *the player*, as his friends used to address him. Little did he know, his heart would be so invested in someone, so deep, and so intense.

'I got fired. That's when it hit me, and I've made changes. I've made progress. It's been a couple of months. But applying for new jobs has become tougher than I envisioned because of the fact that I got fired in my previous job. It is now a black mark on my resume, and new companies are not convinced. Also, my previous company, was one of the best in terms of finance, so it's going to be hard for me now.'

She was quiet... preoccupied.

'Say something, no?'

'Sorry, no... I'm just lost in thought... its good you are making changes. It's very risky if you carry on that way, right?.'

'Well, of course... but once you're in it, easier said than done, I guess. However, I'm in a better headspace. I really miss you. Do you miss me?' he asked in such an honest tone, and the arrow pierced her in the centre of her heart. She missed him, of course, she did. She missed Dev too. The thought twisted her mind; she was surprised she was still thinking of him while sitting with Aarav.

'I do miss you, but I don't know where we stand if you are talking about us being in a relationship again. You were my first, but the space apart has also made me become conscious of so many things about myself. Like, sometimes, things that feel right are probably wrong for me, and vice versa, but I am still figuring it out.'

'Why don't we give it a try, Alisha? I'm not putting pressure, just saying that I'm starting on a clean slate. If I had another chance with you, it would make me feel deserving of the love I received and also the love I have to give you. The space apart has also opened my eyes about a lot of things. Think about it.'

A long silence ensued before they called for the bill. They hugged for a very long goodbye, and Alisha felt drawn to his touch but didn't say anything just yet, though the certainty was felt. She was happy to be in his arms but couldn't admit it to herself or to him.

Chapter 18

Sometimes, things can only be seen from up close.
Sometimes, only from a distance.

The dinner party would commence in a few hours. Alisha had organised most of it and was just waiting for the cake now. It was her parent's silver jubilee, and she wanted to do something nice to entertain them. They never made the effort to do things for themselves, and over the years, their outings were more necessity-oriented. The entire week prior to their silver jubilee, she had planned outings for them and celebrated the week ending with a nice party with their friends. As she was decorating her backyard, she was enthralled by the view of the lights with the backdrop of the mountains…

She had invited many of her parents close friends, including Aarav and Dev's parents. It had been so long. She had personally called Dev and invited him. She wasn't able to understand why she was so eagerly waiting to meet him when it was Aarav who was waiting for her decision. This constant confusion wasn't ideal; it felt like the past was walking into her present. She was so perplexed that she decided to speak to Dr Amar about it in her session before the gathering.

She set up everything and left the house. Her parents would be back by evening. She would return before them, and the guests were invited for 8:30 pm. It would be a grand celebration, and her parents would be so happy. She felt so good about the night.

As she waited for her turn at the clinic, she heard the door open. She looked up and saw Naina. She knew they would meet since she worked there full-time now.

'Hi! We need to stop meeting only in the clinic,' squealed Naina.

'How are you, my dear?' Alisha gave her a warm hug.

They chatted for a few minutes, and the receptionist signalled to Alisha to go in for her appointment.

'Hey, look! I am in a rush, but listen, tonight is my parents' silver jubilee and I've invited all their friends. It'll be great if you can drop in! I know it's really last minute, but please try if you can take some time off... and I had invited Aru, Dev, uncle, and aunty... so we're all going to be there, like old times. Please come if you can! It'll be good fun; we can spend some time together.'

'Aww, thanks, Alisha. I'll try and see if I can drop in for a short while.'

'How are you feeling? Are the panic attacks less frequent?' Dr Amar asked.

The doctor had an assistant who was trying to take notes based on their communication. He had always insisted that his patients understand that anxiety and depression may be mental disorders, but they are very concrete and physical problems that one is dealing with. He had explained to her a few sessions ago how people experience various physical symptoms like stomach upsets, headaches, tremors, and the like. Of course, the difference arises in the fact that some minds are more fragile, and some people get triggered in different ways. Some minds are in constant denial; some are open to gaining awareness. A lot of one's mental health was also co-dependent on the culture they came from, their family backgrounds, and their lifestyle. In that way, it could not be generalised.

The only dangerous part about mind-related problems is that if they are not addressed and taken care of at the right time, they negatively impact others around the person, and that is very difficult to treat. Caregivers go through an equally hard time.

'The attacks are very mild and subdued. I honestly haven't felt like a fish out of water for many months, but I do wonder now if I should stop taking medicines?'

'We will cross that bridge when it comes. I have, anyway, reduced your dosage to half for 3 months. If you feel better, we can aim for that. But there is nothing to worry about. Let's take it one step at a time.'

'Doctor, there was something else I wanted to discuss with you, if I may?'

'Sure.'

'Doctor, you know how I felt when I came to you. You also know that Aarav and I have been keeping our distance, but we met the other day, and we may want to give it another try.'

'If that is something you want, why is it bothering you?'

'Yes, I miss him. But I also don't know if it's the correct thing to get back together. I also really, really miss my friendship with Dev, but I know things will never be the same. What I really want to tell you, is that a certain amount of guilt is really triggering my anxiety. I feel like I am deeply invested in both of them, and that is really not an ideal situation to be in emotionally.'

'Well, of course, it isn't, but it's good you are aware of how you feel. Now it should be a matter of using that awareness to make the right decision. The right decision means safeguarding the emotions of others around you, including yourself....'

As she was walking out, she felt a weight being lifted off her shoulders. It was good to finally understand that she deeply loved both of them, and it was not the best place to be in, but acknowledging that reality made her feel less heavy. A friendship as long as theirs was bound to make her feel this way, and a new, enchanting love was one of its own kind. She wasn't trying to harm anyone. Like a self-confrontation, she was more confident of meeting both of them soon.

Chapter 19

Picture perfect moments are made of triumphs over epochs of working through the struggles.

The magic in the air was the culmination of everyone's positive vibes, combined with their presence. It was a pretty momentous occasion for Alisha's parents, celebrating twenty-five glorious years of ups, downs, and everything in between.

They always wanted only one child, if it was a daughter, and they were definitely proud parents to have someone in their life whom they could call their very own. She had imbibed the best of them, and more than anything else, they had managed to be the best of friends, which was a rare find.

Everyone had gathered for the cake cutting, and the little piñata of confetti had added all the sparkle they needed. Many elderly couples took after her parents on the dance floor. It was so sweet to watch them dance and reminisce their youth.

Alisha looked fabulous in a purple off-shoulder gown. She finally took off her stilettos and walked on the damp grass to serve herself some food before meeting anyone. She was so hungry and preoccupied about the event, she finally felt relieved that she could unwind. She served herself and walked towards an empty table.

'Eating before the guests?!'

'Dev, oh my God!' she jumped and hugged him.

He looked dashing in a black shirt and blue jeans. His hair had grown, and he had a slight stubble. Getting older was totally suiting him!

He hugged her tight. He didn't know when he would, ever again. He had longed for this moment for the last 3 years. To just be in her embrace, even for a few seconds, so he could have that moment to remember.

They slowly separated themselves from each other.

'Oh my God! I knew I would be happy to see you, but I'm overexcited!' With glistening eyes, she continued like the chatterbox she always was. 'I really never thought there would be anything that would change our friendship. I think with everything I've come to accept, this is something I still struggle with, like a lot.'

He pulled the chair close to hers, and they sat down. He helped himself to some of the food from her plate.

'Al, it's not just you. Honestly, it was a bit hard for me too. I didn't know how to suddenly respond to the relationship between Aarav and you. And it felt safer to be away. If I were to stay here, I'm not sure we would be able to be cordial and meet… Think about it. If he kept seeing us on the blue bench, passed by every time we were on the phone together, I didn't know if it would clash with him. Actually, it really would have. We spoke about this a few months ago too… didn't get to explain it to you fully, but this is summarising how I feel, I guess…'

She didn't expect them to get right into it without the artificial formalities, but she was more than glad. Better now than later; they may never even get a chance to clear the air.

'I didn't get you. Why wouldn't we be cordial? I get that it was different because he is your brother, and I have definitely experienced that awkwardness, but I would always be more than cordial with you!'

'No, it's not that. Look. I think I didn't realise how close we were. And I didn't know that, I didn't know at all. It was only when you guys got closer, strange feelings of jealousy and sadness started bubbling inside me. You know me inside out, from when we were kids. To me, sitting with you on that blue bench was the routine. I wasn't even aware that things could ever change, let alone the way they actually did. And don't get me wrong, it isn't anyone's fault, right? Aarav is so charming and has anyway always had a way with people. For me, the realisation hit only after things started changing between our dynamic.'

Alisha was mind-boggled. It was great that they were talking, but this was going at a speed she could not yet process. It felt like he was afraid the others would come to meet them, and they wouldn't get an alone moment, so he just went on and on, and she wasn't able to understand that it was really him pouring his heart out.

'And Alisha, if you come to think of it, being close friends and not being able to spend as much time is hard enough. Imagine you and I are chilling, and Aarav and you have a date at that same time. Like, it would get really weird between all 3 of us. That night… when your voice broke…

I'm sorry I wasn't there for you.' He couldn't understand his lies, but he knew it would be better than telling her the truth.

'Somewhere in the midst of all this, I realised I could not cross a line and come between the 2 of you. I always thought the hardest part about going to live in the hostel would be living away from you, from all my closest friends. You're the closest to me, but it turned out that it became a relief. Because that night made me understand that if I stayed back, I would definitely be coming in between you guys. I would never be able to stay away from you, right? So then the hostel plan became my saviour, and it was so much better to be away, even though the distance was hard. I miss hanging out too, but now we're adults, and we have to be mature about these changes. We will always have each other's back, that goes without saying.'

Alisha slowly comprehended that he was opening up to her a lot because he knew they were not together, she and Aarav. The wave of sadness washed over her again as she remembered what Aarav told her just a few days ago: that he wanted another chance. How could it happen to them all over again?

'Say something,' he nudged.

'I... I,' she couldn't find the words. 'I wondered that night, kept wondering... how come you didn't come when my voice broke. It shocked me. Aarav was very supportive though. In my head, it didn't make sense. How can my best friend, who's practiced a million times with me, not be there after that incident...? I felt abandoned, I kept thinking. But I guess Aarav and I were already in too deep, and when I tried to call you, you avoided me completely… it crushed me. But I get your point. His presence then was the most comforting feeling for me. I found other parts of me, and it helped me ignore the questions, to which I probably didn't want the answers anyway but then…'

Dev was relieved when he heard the *but*…

'But… I didn't know, Dev. It's like I realised I was deeply involved in your life, but I had no idea you felt it too. It all makes sense now, doesn't it… the way you avoided me because you were trying to give us space, now understanding that you found it awkward, and that made it so much easier for me to get closer to Aarav… and when I felt that emptiness that you weren't with me, I tried to reach out… and then you never responded, so I was convinced it was one-sided…it sounds silly now I know… but it wasn't at that point… and that is kind of hard to process right now… this is a lot, right! If you responded to me, we could have spent time the way we used to. I know you feel differently… anyway, let it go. You still haven't told me what you want from me though, remember… *Guitar*…?' He was surprised she remembered, but she obviously couldn't give him what he wanted.

'Well, how about not discussing this topic to keep us both sane?' he laughed. She was offended by the sarcasm, but it made perfect sense in the irony of their situation.

It was just those few minutes they had together, and they were surrounded by all their old friends. Harsh, Anna, and all the others spotted them and pulled up their chairs closer to catch up. They were back to reality and back to pretending like nothing happened. Anyway, nothing did happen.

It was an hour later that Aarav came. He met everyone and joined the table where their friends were.

'Wow, guys, it's like we're back in time, right!'

The revelry shimmered through the night. Alisha noticed that Aarav didn't take a drink. She was happy for him, confused for herself, and hopeless about Dev. She needed a few more minutes with him, but what could she say?

Aarav came over and gently squeezed Alisha's shoulders. It made things very obvious in front of their peer group that they were still deeply in love. Dev got up and started walking towards his parents.

The night was coming to an end as all the guests started saying their goodbyes. Aarav's family didn't move. It was weird, Alisha thought. It was like they wanted to leave in the end.

In the end, it was just their 2 families. They were helping Alisha clear things up, and the boys were chatting with her parents. Aarav's dad came up to her dad, and they signalled everyone to come together.

'Arun, we have known each other for a very long time. Our children have been friends, just like us, and somewhere, I guess we all knew this would turn into a familial bond. I request to seek your permission in pursuing the marriage of our children, of course, only if they both are willing….'

Dev felt like a million arrows struck him all at once. With a stagger, he held the chair and broke into a big, pretentious smile. '*Fake it till you make it*,' he thought. All doors shut on him at the same time.

Aarav smiled, while Alisha stood absolutely blank, and Arun warmly embraced his dad.

Chapter 20

The superfluities need to be removed to find the profoundness of simplicity.

'This is beyond ridiculous!' Alisha screamed as if she was mortified.

Her parents were in a daze. They had never seen her this way. This wasn't a panic attack; she was in a rage.

'How on Earth could you agree to this without even having the conversation with me? What are we living in, the 1600s?'

'Calm down, Alisha!' Asha screamed back. 'We have never stopped you from making any decisions. We thought this is what you want, and we even overheard you and Aarav discussing the future on one of your calls! It's stupid of you to doubt us! And it's much better you'll settle down than do this make-up, break-up rubbish! We know how you youngsters get fickle!'

'Whaaaat? What we speak is private, mum.'

It really stung both her parents. They genuinely thought they were making her happy, and this was probably the way she wanted things to go. It was the right way to approach the topic as well. *Did they just really goof up by not discussing it with her prior?* They were under the assumption that it was pre-discussed between the kids, and they thought they were making things much easier.

'Alisha!! You have been pining for him ever since your break-up. Why are you behaving like you are in love with someone else, or you are against the idea of marriage all of a sudden?'

She didn't know what to say; she was coming across as hypocritical. In seconds, she felt the whole room spinning around her and burst into tears as she sank into the bean bag in her living room. Her parents gave her a few moments to calm down. It was true, her mind told her. Why was she behaving this way? She knew she wanted to marry early, and with Aarav and his family, there would never be restrictions on her lifestyle or whether she wanted to work, etc. What was her problem? It was hard to face and admit it to her parents, but she had to admit it to herself at some point, she thought…

'What is it, Alisha? Why are you being impossible and making it sound like we are against your wishes or something? And anyway, if this is what is on your mind, clearly we have read you all wrong, and I will call them and say sorry, cancel it right away… you don't have to feel so pressurised,' her dad stated.

Alisha fumbled for words…

'Sorry, Mum, dad… I don't know what it is, it's complicated… but there are things on my mind, and maybe I didn't feel like this is going to happen just yet. It would have been less of a shock if you had told me. It felt so filmy and stupid.'

'There is something else bothering you, baby... out with it, please,' her mum urged.

'It is complicated... like I don't know how Dev will take it. *They should have guessed.* Ever since Aarav and I got together, we barely get time to even hang out together. I sometimes wonder if we were not dating, would he have shifted to the hostel. Would he still be close to me like he used to? I guess part of me is still scared to face that. And to be an *official* part of their family means I have to live this fear that Dev would never be ok with us being married. Dating someone and spending time is one thing; being a part of their family would be completely different, right? I guess I just want to make sure he is ok with this, and none of this was expected, so I'm wondering how he's taken it! I feel like I should have given him a heads up, but I only didn't know....it was so weird.'

There was a long silence. They thought about it. They sat for their dinner and wound up the evening. No one said anything. It was making Asha uncomfortable; she sensed Alisha was confused with both the brothers, and that was not an ideal situation. Arun was tensed because he didn't want to make a decision for the present, risking disharmony in their future. There was an air of dishonesty, even though no one acknowledged it. It was too delicate a situation to comment on.

It was 2 am when Alisha went to her parent's room and snuggled between them, like she did when she was a child.

Her pillow was wet with tears of confusion. She wanted to tell them about his drinking… she couldn't get herself to. He promised her he would change his ways and requested her not to bring this up because then her parents would tell his parents. She hated this manipulation, but she also felt like she should give him a chance. Hiding things from her parents never felt right, and she didn't know how to spring this on them after all that was already going on.

Her parents were restless, not knowing what to make of the situation. It is not that they doubted the love between Aarav and Alisha, but the fact that she had such an intense meltdown and absurd reaction only meant that there was more to what met the eye. And living together, sometimes, could become saturating if people didn't express themselves clearly or set their emotional boundaries right. They didn't want to push their daughter into something that she would not be okay with later, but there was no way to be sure about what she wanted. They also knew she would not want to be married to anyone apart from Aarav.

Maybe they should just postpone the next meeting with them or just buy time till they were sure? They wondered if their parents knew these details. Boys don't express as much to their parents, or was he wrong?

But, what if Aarav found someone else in that time?

Bizarre scenarios and thoughts circled their minds until they drifted into a deep sleep.

Chapter 21

The knock on the door was loud. Alisha scrambled, being half asleep, and opened the door. She was surprised to find Dev standing there with his suitcase.

'What a surprise! Come inside.'

'Thanks, good morning too!' he smiled.

'What brings you here? Gosh, it's like the clock has rewound....'

Why is he smiling so much? So weird after what happened last night, she thought to herself.

'Well, I knew our parents are together, and you would be home alone. Aarav has gone for his job interview...I was leaving for the hostel, thought I'd say a quick hi and bye...what since we left our conversation unfinished last evening, and now I guess congratulations are in order?' he spoke fast.

'Dev, there was a major scene at home yesterday,' she said softly and sank back into the bean bag again.

She thought his eyes were teary, but she couldn't tell for sure.

'Why, isn't it what you want anyway?'

'Well, it isn't so simple. I acknowledged it to my parents too... officially being a part of your family is going to be very delicate. And things are already so different with you and me. Aarav and I are just about rediscovering ourselves out of the relationship and trying to get back in one. It's strange for me too. I know you think I have told you enough, but it was very hard for me when you and I couldn't be as close as we were, and after you said those things to me last night, it got me thinking. I can't even understand my own feelings. I am so deeply invested in both of you, and it isn't a great situation to jump into marriage, don't you think?'

'Let's keep it clear, Al. These conversations just keep us going in circles. We cannot keep repeating ourselves, right? I already told you, for me, it is a no-brainer. And I'm not going to be the reason you and Aarav don't get together, right? It's complicated, no doubt, but since we both have awareness, we will figure it out in time. We will learn to live with this different kind of love that doesn't need to be expressed and acted on. I will always care about you, that goes without saying….'

'It can't be so simple. I'll be in that house. How is it going to be okay? Am I being immoral…a bad person? What is all this confusion? Why is it so complicated? If you and I are best friends, then why is it that we don't even talk much anymore? Does this feel wrong on some level, or am I being delusional? I don't know.'

'Stop being so melodramatic, now leave it. All this is just a play of words and thoughts. What is wrong and immoral?

Things just happened organically with you 2, and you and I go way back in time…

'He is your first love. I am your best friend. It is just the way it was meant to unfold, and things change; it is the only constant, right? Now, please, take a deep breath, go with the flow.'

Alisha was not surprised at him always being more mature than the other friends she had, but this much mindfulness was a lot to absorb. It was an unsaid approval that she was silently waiting for. Now, the guilt would subside, and she could probably move ahead in her mind and start afresh, having the best of both worlds.

Chapter 22

The wedding was quite a grand affair at the Willow Banks Hotel. The scenic outdoors were the perfect place to capture the precious union of souls. Alisha wore a baby pink sari with heavy embroidery and a simple tube blouse. She looked undeniably gorgeous. Aarav looked subtle and handsome in his black and white suit, and Dev did a great job hiding his crestfallen heart. The festivities and celebrations were inaudible to his innocent heart. Luckily, Naina was a pillar of support for him; she heard him out umpteen number of times, circling back to the same sentence at the end of every breakdown – 'I wish I had told her first...'

What made it harder for him was the fact that she stuck to Aarav. I mean, obviously, what was he expecting? They had been together, broken up, and gotten back. Even if they were not together, it would be ridiculous to switch brothers – something that would be impossible, a thought which would be deeply unappreciated by them and their families too. What was he thinking? Had he gone crazy? But in some deep corner of his heart, he held onto the secret for so long because he knew he couldn't have her... and when he finally mustered up that courageous moment to be able to tell her, he obviously chose not to. What was the use? He would just confuse her. It would have been much better for him to have stayed back in the hostel. This was too difficult, attending their wedding!

It was obvious that he had hoped for them to be together, and now, to accept that he had to be a part of their wedding was not making sense to him. He was rubbing salt on his own wounds… downright broken-hearted, even though he knew he wasn't making any sense.

'Aarav, don't mess this up,' Harsh was giving him a mature talk while helping him get ready. 'Look, not everyone gets another chance. Alisha is sorted as a person; don't go and make a mess of things, not after she has been upfront with you about what she wants and doesn't. It is a huge deal for her not telling her parents about your habits; please do not let her down.'

Aarav was already intoxicated and promised Harsh he would quit lying from now on. Harsh was quite worried about the debacle that would follow if Alisha found out. He made him a coffee, gave him a bottle of mouthwash, shook him up, and spoke to him at length. When he sensed he was hitting a roadblock, he yelled at him.

'You know what, Aarav? Go, go screw it up. She should have rather married your brother!' he screamed and stormed out of the room.

That shook Aarav from within. He never had the thought of them being together in that way, ever.

Minutes later, when Dev saw the spectacle of Aarav gathering himself together, he felt a deep sense of remorse.

'I'm done with your lies, Aarav. I'm going to tell her everything. This is bullshit.'

'Dev. It's our wedding day. Buzz off before it gets out of hand. You don't need to bloody interfere.'

'You are lying to her, through and through. She doesn't deserve you!' he yelled back.

'And with your lies, you are again dragging me down. Don't you remember how upset she was when she found out I knew? This time you have played us all. You told us all you are clean. What the hell is even going on today and why?'

'What the hell is your problem? Are you in love with her?' he stared with anger.

'Would that make any difference to you? Yes, I am. Now, what are you going to do?'

Aarav raced towards him with his hands clenched in a fist. He punched forward when Dev held it tight. His parents appeared at that very instant and stared in shock. They had zero idea of what was happening.

Dev was grief-stricken. He couldn't understand where to draw the line between interfering and not. He was disgusted with himself and his lack of priorities, his inability to protect Alisha, and the damage he would cause if he opened his mouth. In sheer helplessness, he left the venue without attending the wedding. By the time they would notice, he would say he had an immediate assessment at the hostel.

But, Alisha didn't know anything. By the time the formalities ended, Aarav was quite alright. The bliss of being newlyweds had engulfed her mind and body. She made a conscious effort to put the past behind her and start a brand new day. Aarav loved her intensely; if only he knew himself without his addictions…

The families were in a state of ecstasy and happiness. The joy spread in the air. Amidst the festivities, Alisha did notice that Dev was gone. Even though her heart refused to let go and stop thinking about him, her mind let go completely. She knew it would be a matter of a few days until he would come home, the same home in which she would stay too, with Aarav.

PART THREE

Chapter 1

Present Day, about 6 years later.

We will all see the light, one flicker at a time.

He held his brother's hand and went towards the car. The last 6 months were very difficult for Dev. He had just started practising at the IGMC hospital, and it was difficult to keep the balance between home and work. He had returned from the hostel a year ago, and things were already deteriorating between Aarav and Alisha. Her pleading eyes didn't have to speak any words for him to try his best to fix things between the 2 of them. That's why, with the help of Naina and some senior colleagues, he was able to curate a specialised rehabilitation programme at IGMC itself, something that was never done before.

Aarav was obviously reluctant to go, but his ways had got the better of him, and it was him against 4 adults at home; he didn't have a choice. Sara was young, and Alisha was close to a mental breakdown with his erratic behaviour and drunkenness. Barely a year into their wedding, she realised he hadn't changed his ways at all; he would either make excuses to stay out till late, or he would pretend to be a social drinker but would appear at the event already deeply intoxicated. They even saw Dr Amar, the renowned doctor who really helped Alisha get a grip on herself, but Aarav wasn't ready to receive any guidance. His parents attended meetings with him too, trying to search for answers from his childhood or adolescence that had probably led him to be so haywire. But nothing fit the puzzle, and no reasoning was suitable to understand what he wanted, or to justify his behaviour. How he went from being head boy to a completely headless boy was a mystery.

Aarav, on the contrary, did not even have the awareness of what was happening to the others because of him. His was just a fun addiction, and he was so involved in it, so much so that he was oblivious to the struggle he was creating. Sara was just 4 years old, and Aarav was fascinated but kept a distance; he wasn't as involved a father as Alisha would have liked him to be, or generally how dads should be. He had changed 3 jobs in the last 2 years, and the final job he got was with a lot of help from his ex-colleagues. It was a night shift client relations manager, and it just worsened the entire routine.

Dev and Alisha met outside their home many a time to figure out the course of his reintegration. They could not speak freely at home, fearing that Aarav would not approve of the plotting and planning. Uncle and aunty had faith in Dev's choices for Aarav's recovery. He was alienating himself from everyone without realising it. There was a time when they were seated in the café near their school, and the mountain backdrop and cold wind reminded them both of their younger days, the light-heartedness, and carefree times they had grown up with. Growing up was rather overrated. While trying to comfort her, Dev put his hand on Alisha's, and she held it tight. A sudden twinge of discomfort made her stand up from her chair. The line was blurry between what they shared and what they felt.

'It's a matter of 3 to 6 months, Al. He will detox, and only then will he be able to gain perspective. This coming and going weekly isn't showing great results; he treats it like a formality. He just avoids questions, makes false promises. He doesn't care... nothing has rocked the boat. He takes everything for granted. Such a situation cannot be cured with just weekly visits. He needs a proper 360-degree turnaround. And that can only happen if he is physically in a clean, green space, away from all substances. He needs clean food and clean conversations, a clean mind, and clarity. He needs a fresh slate to restart.'

'What do I tell Sara?' she sounded irritated. 'I know she is a kid, but I can't just tell her he is vacationing for 6 months, right!'

'She is small, there is no need to discuss much. Even if you try saying anything, she is obviously not going to grasp the depth of anything, no? We will say some work-related stuff. Besides, we all are at home together, and you can go and stay at your folks place for a while too. She will be easily distracted. But the IGMC faculty may need your input from time to time, so you consider how much you have left in you to help this relationship recoup. They will ask you most of the questions since you are his wife. Then they will ask us too, but for the current details, you will have a lot of information to share with them.'

She took a deep breath. There was so much going on with her right now. She was trying to move forward with her music. With great difficulty, convincing and persuasion from Sir Anthony, she agreed to participate in the Nationals of the Voice of India competition. It had been a few years since she had not taken part in anything big, and her family thought this would be a great way to buy her some sanity. The studio was so accommodating, they even allowed her to bring her daughter to her practice sessions in the studio so she would not have to rush back or worry about her. There was a lot she had hidden from the family about Aarav, about his erratic ways and illogical reasoning. That should have been her signal that things were not meant to be, hiding from her parents always made her feel like she was treading on the wrong path. It was only *Dev* from both the families who knew her, him, and the entire situation inside out. She was wondering how she would cope with him being in a facility, even though this is precisely what she wanted for him and it was exactly what he needed.

'Ok, let's do this…' she sighed.

Chapter 2

The beautiful irony of setting boundaries is that it
sets you free.

It had been a few years since Alisha had been off medication. She was dedicated to her treatment, and she didn't feel as helpless as she did in her teenage and early adult years. She had learnt various coping methods, and in retrospect, she was grateful she had gone through that phase before she got married. With her current circumstances, it would not help if she too was dealing with a personal crisis. It is not that difficult to get help.

That's the thing about life: we don't realise what is bothering us half the time. Our reactions are so embedded in us that, 9 out of 10 times, we are responding to something within us, not to the situation at hand.

And that is something only a small percentage of people are able to understand, including the few who have attained a high level of awareness and are trying to help society through various ways.

Be it in organisations, businesses or relationships, getting the balance of power between 2 viewpoints is close to impossible. Whichever angle the power tilts towards, that person/organisation/relationship tends to win over the situation, without concern as to whether it is the right or wrong thing.

The reason behind these irrationalities is the repressed and unexpressed trauma that we have gone through at various stages of our life, and when the right emotion is not expressed in the right way at the right time on a right platform, it obviously convulses into whichever form it finds an expression in.

So, to assume we all have to respond in that perfect reaction is also irrational because then, instead of being human beings, we would be a clan of perfectly charged robots. But what we can do (and are not doing) as the human race is to give a basic structure and platform for humans to exist, a rough idea as to what is okay and not okay, and it is only when people start practising basic respect and balance in their close relationships can we expect the ripples to pass through and help with communities, cities, and then countries.

Like charity begins at home, even clarity begins at home.

Naina's article was published in the Foray Magazine, which was an annual magazine put together by the IGMC faculty. Alisha was intrigued by her writing.

She was lost in thought, sipping her coffee in the lobby for a while, when Dev gently patted her shoulder. She wanted to share her opinions on this with him; he was the only one in her life who understood her in a way that she didn't have to explain herself to be understood. Their chemistry was electric, it was sad it fizzled out.

'Come, you have some forms to fill. I tried my best to not make it a rigorous rehab routine. He'll get a lot of chill time and a lot of counselling, to which he has to respond to, so I don't know how long that will take. But de-addiction is a process, and you will need to put all your anger and frustration aside if you want to see changes in him. I'm setting it up for 6 months.'

Alisha stared at him, irritated and signed the forms.

'You guys at home deal with him for 10 minutes a day, and everyone is already harrowed, but I am supposed to put all my emotions aside to see changes in him? So convenient!'

Aarav was in the waiting room. Exactly a year ago, he had brought the roof down when they suggested a rehabilitation centre, and it was since then that Alisha had, for the very first time in their relationship, put her foot down to the extreme of leaving him. She was so saturated and had made up her mind to not tolerate any of this anymore. What was the point in filling a cup with a hole at the bottom? That's when Aarav got a partial reality check, and in the weeks that ensued, he realised that sooner or later, if he didn't agree to this, she would leave him. He wasn't scared of that when he was drinking or smoking, but the few sober hours in between made him feel very restless, and he knew that retaliation in any form would anyway lead him there forcefully.

He didn't have a job anymore, obviously.

Alisha went inside the waiting room and sat down. Aarav pulled his chair close to hers. Dev left the room to give them some space to speak alone.

How is it that I still feel heartbroken? He thought to himself.

'Look... I...' Aarav stammered.

'Don't... just don't say anything. You remember years ago when I wanted to end things between us? I always, always knew this was not a good idea. I just don't have the answers as to why I let it go on and didn't stop it at the right time. Love is not enough to sustain a marriage. Here we are, trapped in the same web. I've decided this is the last time trying for me, Aarav. I'll be there for you, but not at the cost of losing myself. I will figure things out. Even if *you* keep making the same choices, I won't. Take care. I'll come every morning to meet you. I need to head to the studio now.'

Her heart was pounding, and she felt like a bad person for having been so stern with him, but she knew if she didn't give him a dose of the truth, he would not take it seriously. There was no point in being spun in the same web anymore. They had to break free, at least one of them did.

How much courage it required, she thought. *Here she was, ready to represent her state in the national singing competition, but these confrontations with Aarav scared her much more. And she couldn't really tell why. Was she afraid of not being a so-called 'good spouse' who constantly tolerated emotions she could not handle? Or was it a generational habit for women to subdue themselves more than required?* Alisha was too confounded by her own behaviour and decided it best not to further analyse her riotous mind.

Chapter 3

The studio had gone through a full renovation. The white walls were now a light shade of off-white, and an entire section was decorated with graffiti, which had been painted by all the students and faculty themselves. They had decided to paint it in a theme of all their favourite songs by their favourite artists. That would be a great way to add a personal touch to their space.

It was the most fun phase of the previous month. They got together every night, ordered food and drinks from outside, and painted like kids in their overalls. It fostered a deep sense of friendship and harmony between all of them, and it felt blessed to have created a little family of their own.

Each of them participated in different competitions; some just came for training, and some to train others with their passions. It was a great creative space for people to share, learn, express, and hone talents.

Alisha also urged Sir to set aside some space in the front for a huge shelved wall of fame. The idea occurred to her post the nationals when 3 of them from the academy had taken part. They didn't make it as winners, but the recognition and exposure were quite an experience. She made the suggestion to put up everyone's achievements on the wall so as to remind old students of their potential and to inspire new students who enrolled. They were disappointed when they didn't win the nationals, but they also knew it was no easy task, and the training would have to increase manifold to be able to make a mark on that level. They were all geared up to participate again the following year.

Anthony Sir had recruited more help. He was getting old and wanted motivators for his students. He also introduced instrument classes to give the singers a holistic experience and their own opportunities to start a band if they wished to. Musical equipment, speakers, subwoofers, karaoke sets, and a host of new things were brought in post the renovation. It was a brand new arena compared to what it was when Alisha was younger.

Career-wise, Alisha would reach her peak if she won this, as the studio was one of its kind in the state and had received so much recognition over the years. It was a distant dream, one she wished for with open and closed eyes.

The national level competitions were not just single song performances; they were multiple performances on the same day with different categories such as acoustic, duet, own creativity, a medley, and finally an individual performance. She had alot of work to do individually and with her teammates. Often, her parents would drop Sara to the studio, and she thoroughly enjoyed the ambience. Music was inbuilt in some people, and Alisha hoped her little one could enjoy the beauty and sheer magic that music brought to one's life.

'This is the road to big platforms, Alisha. Taking part in India's Nightingale,' Sir had told her time and again. Performing internationally (if she made it through any national podium) was beyond her imaginings, but there was no point in not trying. At the most, she wouldn't make it. But in the midst of a broken marriage, finding her voice was arduous. Despite this being her only solace, it was also not easy to compete with top-notch singers. She was taking one step at a time. For now, winning the nationals would be great. Even second place wasn't going to bring her a spot to the international stage. But on the bright side, the top 5 contestants would get signed up with different record companies, within India, which would be a fantastic opportunity to begin with!'

Chapter 4

The only way out is within.

The rehabilitation programme was monotonous and rigorous. It was a miracle they had got him here, but Aarav was restless most of the time. They had taken away his phone, left him with a book and pen, and asked him to write down his feelings. '*Write down my feelings? What the hell?*' he thought. His frustration had grown manifold. His food was supervised, timings were to be adhered to, and it was basic hell for a free spirit like him, except that he had caged himself in his own freedom and ended up there.

The only ray of light in his darkness was meeting her in the mornings. But she was so saturated with him, she barely spoke. She came like a formality, and he was very conscious in the new environment. She was a few weeks into her second pregnancy, and her hormones were all over the place. She was wondering how she would manage it all; the tension was taking a toll on her.

The weekends were slightly better as he got to meet his daughter. It was strange because back home, he never made an effort to spend time with her, but those few moments he got now, he began to cherish. So typical and clichéd of human beings to not value what they have when it is in front of them and to crave the same when they are separated from it. He promised himself that he would mend his ways. Alisha wouldn't share her excitement with him this time the way she did when she was carrying Sara. He realised he was losing out on a lot. It was a matter of time. If he didn't take responsibility for his actions, everything would slip out of his hands, and his family would be taken care of by his brother and his parents.

'Why are you here, pa?' Sara would ask every weekend. 'When will you come home? Do you like it here? Shall I bring you games and chocolate?'

It was like the bad movies. He had no idea how he got himself into this.

Dev brought Sara on the weekends, along with their parents. Alisha would come on the weekdays. He initially complained a lot, but over the weeks, he figured out that he had no backing to get out. The only way out now was to go within and rectify his rather ignorant and arrogant self.

'It's like a fancy prison,' he complained to Dev.

'Be happy you're not in an actual one, idiot,' he replied angrily.

Dev couldn't understand his older brother. What was he always on about? Why couldn't he value what he had? Why was he always so flippant? The counselling team made no discoveries as to why he was this way, but they managed to make him understand that this was not the way forward. To what had started this, they had no answers. Dev used to look up to Aarav, but what had he been looking up to?

Chapter 5

'Come on, Anthony Sir, Alisha requested. Let me take over. I have some free time when I come here anyway, and I'll be more than glad to help you out.'

'You already have your plate full. What more do you want to do? There is no need to further exert yourself.'

'I could use some distractions. Besides, it is just for a few months, and it'll count as my training too. In the ninth month, I will definitely take a long break Sir… let me handle it, you relax…'

There was no way to convince Alisha when she made up her mind. Sir had a batch of newbies to train, and he was rather held up with organising event after event. He barely got time to train the contestants who were participating in higher level competitions. She wanted to chip in and help so he could concentrate on assisting his older students, and she was happy to take up the new batch. New energies and new talents – it would be a fun way to spend her time too, she thought.

'How will you handle Sara?'

'She will be more than happy to see new faces here, Sir! Trust me, we've got this!'

The next day, she had enrolled 9 new students to the academy, a mixed age group. Over the years in the studio, they had put in all their ideas to curate new forms of training.

People get nervous while training, so, to bring out their confidence and to provide comfort, pairing them in groups initially makes them feel a lot less nervous. Alisha herself had drawn from that experience. Her competition with Sanjay was the most enjoyable and supportive; it boosted her morale in so many ways.

Partaking from her own learnings, she conducted joint sessions with the students, helping them showcase their flairs in a freestyle initially before helping them channelize their strengths into their particular specialties. She spent a lot of quality time with each of them individually post the sessions to get to know them better and give them tips from her expertise and experiences over the years. Learning and sharing anything related to music was the most peaceful form of expression for her. In that space, she forgot everything and lived idealistically, unpretentiously, and so happily.

Chapter 6

Alisha reached the centre an hour late. He was waiting impatiently, unable to sip on his coffee. Coffee was a rare treat; limiting caffeine for a while was one of the suggestions. Although he looked forward to it once in a few days, he was still not able to enjoy it.

'What took you so long today? I was waiting to meet you.'

'Why? Aren't you tired of the same old rubbish we keep getting into? Don't you appreciate this breath of fresh air without all our baggage?' she snapped.

She never knew this side of herself, and neither did he. Rude, agitated, snappy. The Alisha they both knew was mellow, gentle, and always had the aura of elegance. Maybe he drove her to being this version of herself, he thought.

Circumstances have a way of showing us different parts of ourselves.

'Enough, ya! It's hard enough being away from all of you in the first place. The little time we get also you keep talking like this...' he retorted.

'What nonsense are you talking? Just listen to yourself. When you had us, you didn't even pay attention to any of it, so don't start believing the lies your mind is telling you.'

'For God's sake, Alisha, I am TRYING!'

'NO AARAV! We are trying. You weren't even agreeing. Stop, just stop believing your narrative, Aarav. Get real, for once.'

She continued, 'Do you know how hard this has been on your parents, on your brother, on Saru, on me? Do you think at all? I understand everyone has a right to live on their own terms, but what part of this is fair when you choose to drown and make all of us drown with you? I am not so strong; I cannot fight society. However liberal a thinker I am, I'm still scared to scar my kids for no fault of theirs. I'm afraid to break away because I don't know myself without this. But how much to compromise? There should be some respect left, right? Every single time you resort to lying, you don't want to be there for us, and then you get to be a victim sitting in a rehab centre. Be fortunate you got this opportunity. I really don't know how, but you are one lucky man who keeps getting so many chances to make things right. Others have to suffer the wrongs which are not even done by them. Have you ever thought of how this has strained my relationship with my folks? I used to be able to tell them every little thing. When they finally got to know about your habits, they couldn't believe I hid such a thing from them. You've turned it all upside down for me, Aru! It should not be this hard to make simple choices. You want 2 things that don't belong together; you're trying to glue opposite poles. It isn't going to happen.'

There was nothing left to say, and she didn't feel bad about being harsh anymore. He needed to hear this time and again, and only if it sank into him, there would probably be hope from his end to get his act together.

She left in a few minutes. She met the nurse in charge before leaving the premises.

'He is doing better, ma'am. Much better than the first 4 weeks. He isn't fighting with us anymore. But he hasn't opened up; he doesn't speak about his life. He only mentioned his friend, Akshay. I think it is where his addiction started. He said they were not in touch anymore.'

She felt jitters hearing his name. The *power* that name had on Aarav was the road to disaster for him, repeatedly. She wondered how he was... With a shuddering feeling, she left the place. He had got himself into trouble with the authorities... that was the last she knew.

Her visit to the gynaecologist was scheduled for the next day, and Sara was jumping with excitement.

'I think I'm going to have a brother, Mama,' she clapped.

'But you may have a sister too. How would you know, doll?' They were putting together the pieces of her favourite puzzles.

'No, mama, there is a brother in your tummy,' she giggled. 'His name is Nicky!'

Alisha smiled and hugged her baby. What a magical girl she was, always lighting up every little thing around her.

She recalled the day they named her... 'It means *princess*,' Aarav was stroking her forehead and reading out names for her to choose.

'Saisha?'

'No, no, it rhymes with Alisha!'

'Nikita?'

'So common, don't you feel?'

'How about Sara?'

The sound of that struck a chord with both of them... happier times... she reflected. She felt bad now, maybe Dev was right, and she probably did need to put her anger and resentment aside if she wanted to see changes in him. It was like they were stuck in the same repetitive pattern, and only if one of them broke it, the other could behave differently. And between the 2 of them, she had more awareness. She would have to take the first step.

Chapter 7

Learning something is easy;
implementing it is the challenge.

'It is the last trimester, please don't exert yourself too much,' Dr Megha, her gynaecologist, was giving her the routine check-up and advice.

'I'm not able to sing, doctor. I get breathless easily. Is that normal?' she enquired, worriedly.

'Yes, very normal. It's either hormonal changes or digestive issues. If it is hormonal, your voice may take time to return to normal. As the baby is growing, there is more pressure on your abdomen, and your diaphragm. This causes slower digestion, which in turn makes you feel full or bloated. Sometimes, that could be the reason you're feeling breathless. Everything else seems to be ok.'

'But, doctor, I am training for a competition in a few months. If I am not able to sing...'

'Don't worry, Alisha. Train as much as you can, but if you feel discomfort, you may want to rethink it. You take a call based on how you feel.'

She didn't know what to do. The last thing she needed was to stand on stage and have her voice not cooperate, again.

She was confused. Maybe she should try for India's Nightingale the next time? It was held every 2 years. It overwhelmed her because she was so close to the competition date and had trained so long for it.

From her first experience with failure, when she had just started, she had come a long way. The recognitions she received over time had boosted her confidence, and she knew she had gotten way better at her craft. It was a strong passion inside of her, and she wanted to take this big step forward to make a bigger mark.

She went to the studio. She had called in late because of her appointment.

They had a fun session together. Alisha had split them into groups and asked them to sing duets. They all had access to background music now, which gave them an actual experience of singing with the music. When Alisha had joined the studio many moons ago, it was just the students singing and Anthony Sir on either the piano or guitar! Simpler times… she smiled to herself.

As she was orchestrating the last performance, she could see all her students in her batch waving at someone on the other side of the glass door. When she turned around, she was pleasantly surprised. There stood Sanjay, holding his debut album in his hand, with a beaming smile.

'Congratulations!' she squealed in excitement. 'Oh my, creating history and all, huh?'

She knew he was going to pay a visit on one of the days; she just didn't know when. The whole class took a break and went on to congratulate their senior. The younger students went outside, bought a bouquet and cake, and made him cut it, too! It was an entertaining afternoon, and after they dispersed into their practice sessions, Alisha and Sanjay sat in the lobby.

'Wow, Sanju! I'm so excited to hear it! Thanks for giving me the first copy!' she beamed with pride and affection.

'You are most welcome!'

'How did your family react?'

'Well, they are better now. I can't say they are supportive just yet, but at least they don't give me a hard time. Thanks to Amrita *(his sister)*, they are pretending to be understanding, I guess! She has really stood by me, Al. Without her, I don't think I would have been able to get this far.'

'That is so sweet of her! She must love you dearly! I'm sure it's a matter of time before they come around. You guys have such an intense academic background. I think when elderly parents see their children taking new paths, they sort of panic. I don't think they are intentionally unsupportive or anything. Anyway, how did you get to sign the album? Tell me everything and refer me too when I'm ready!' she spoke excitedly.

'That goes without saying,' he smiled. 'You are already a star, Alisha! Check out track number 8, our studio recording cover version of Where Do I Begin….'

Alisha was totally taken aback! She didn't expect this and couldn't believe her eyes. It took a few moments for her to register what he was saying. That was such a sweet gesture, she was totally surprised!

'I'm so thrilled! Thank you for making me a part of this! It's so exciting!'

'Thank you for being such an important part of my journey.' He explained to her the entire process of how the production company got in touch with him, how they released voice-overs in the beginning, and based on the recommendation of his close acquaintance from school, who was the son of a London-based director of music, they pulled some strings and ta-da! Sanjay's debut album was going to be out – *OptiMystic*, is what he called it.

'Love the name! So creative.'

'Ok, enough about me. What's up? How's the bun in the oven?'

'All good! Saru is too excited. She can't wait and has decided it is a boy and should be named Nicky!'

They laughed.

'How is Aarav, Dev?' he asked, wondering if he was crossing a line.

He knew a little about it, not everything.

'He is getting better, thankfully. Dev is good, busy with work. He's a biochemist now, started practising at IGMC and all of that.'

She kept it brief. She could feel herself perspiring.

'And, how are you?'

'I'm... I don't know, Sanjay. I was off meds since the time I got married, but now, for a year, I restarted it. I wasn't in the finest place in my head. It's difficult because I have to be off it again; I cannot do this during my pregnancy, but I'm not feeling the best, been better...'

'Are you in touch with Dr Amar?'

'Yes, now more often. In fact, I have an appointment with him in the coming week.'

'And I heard you submitted your application for India's Nightingale? Congrats, that is huge! Have you heard from them yet?'

'Well, yes, I did. We were to initiate it, but I can't seem to find my voice. I get breathless, and I can't sing right now. I don't know if it is hormonal or what, but I may need to postpone it… next time maybe...'

'Oh.'

He knew this was her ultimate dream.

'It will be when it is meant to be,' he said. 'And don't worry, there are many other ways to get your voice out, not only competitions. I know you will ace whatever you try, but I'm just saying there are other platforms for recognition too, and now that I have some idea and some contacts, I will be happy to network for you.'

His encouragement at that point was much needed, and she felt a lot better.

Chapter 8

Hold on a while, silent and strong,
Nothing is right, nothing is wrong.

'Dev, I think the HOD wants to see you.' The department in charge had called him.

The Head of Department of Research Sciences had called for the annual meeting to discuss the work done in the year. The conference was to be held in Shimla itself that year, putting a lot of work on the IGMC faculty. They even had to create an entertainment segment to keep it lively, and none of the professors were able to curate it, so they were thinking of hiring an event managing company and needed to discuss the budget.

Mr. Sharma, the current HOD, was a tall man with a keen eye for detail. When Dev had begun his internship, he was really confident because he always did well in his assessments and exams, but it was Mr. Sharma who had given Dev a hell of a time, contradicting his assumptions, challenging his answers, and making him rewrite his entire thesis. That was a mammoth task and he wasn't prepared to do it all over again. Dev was at the point of changing his whole career stream when his thesis finally got approved and he was asked to even publish it in the university archives and libraries.

'He will try to see how much pressure you can take,' Naina had told him.

'But that is not the correct way; some of us can really crumble.'

'When you become HOD, make the necessary changes to the system, please,' she had joked with him months ago about it, but she meant what she said about the system needing a change. *The system really needed a change.* This monotonous way of pressurising people was just not right. There had to be a better way to tap into one's potential, a framework which was less rigid and more complacent. This stiff regimen was quite outdated; there were many new options which they could incorporate for assessments and definitely needed to move with the times, they felt.

Since then, for Dev, it was a smoother ride, a more focused approach, and a busy schedule.

'You called me in, Sir?'

'Dev, yes. Please sit down. Give me a moment.'

He was rummaging through some papers when he took a form and handed it over to Dev.

'Please fill this in if you are interested. It is to take over as the Head of Department, as I'm about to retire this year.'

He was stumped. He knew he was good with his work, but heading an entire department was an honour, especially at his age, in this prestigious institution. *'Did Naina have a hand in this?' he thought to himself.* He didn't want to immediately accept it with excitement. Him being him, he wanted to contemplate, weigh out the pros and cons, and then decide.

'You don't look too happy!' he looked serious.

'I am, I am honoured, Sir. I just didn't expect it. Before committing, I would like to sleep over it, Sir. I would not want to take up something without doing justice to it. You set the bar really high.'

'Thank you, son. But this is a joint committee vote; it is not just me alone who thinks you are qualified and prepared to take up this eminent standing. But nevertheless, it is a choice. If you are apprehensive, we will subcontract someone. Let me know in forty-eight hours.'

'For sure, Sir.'

Dev wanted to spend the rest of the day at Dorje Drak. But first, he had to make a quick stop at the rehabilitation quarters, which were behind the campus.

He wanted to go on his routine check to see his brother, who would, anyway, give him a cold vibe. But he did his duty every time he was on the premises.

Aarav despised Dev. Being the younger one and having so much control over his life, he hated the fact that he was literally dancing to his tunes. He didn't realise at that point that this was his path to recovery, a chance at having a real relationship with his wife and children.

He would never know the sacrifices each person in his family had to make to see him through this. He was selfish, he lived for himself… which would not be a bad thing at all, but stagnating the lives of others for one's own whims, that was not fair. He didn't have the awareness that our actions impacted those around us and that each one of us had to assume a certain responsibility towards our family members.

But, that was Aarav. He didn't have an internal radar to guide him through.

He remembered those crazy nights with Akshay and the gang, all the ladies flocking towards him, showering him with needless attention. And even though he was in a committed relationship, he thrived on extra attention. He didn't cross his line, but it definitely satisfied his self-image of being 'cool'. His use of substances became abusive. He knew it was going to get messy, but he always played it casual and blended in with all of them, even though he was senior to their whole gang.

Sometimes he had these thoughts to tell them, *'look guys, this may get a bit dangerous'* or *'I think we should look for some other ways to have fun'*… those feelings did come to his mind many a time, but he always succumbed to peer pressure. Where there was great company, good music, bad habits, and blinding lights, everything else drowned out his inner voices. *'Tomorrow onwards I'll be sober…'* He used to convince himself.

But standing there in that almost empty seventy-five square foot room, it dawned on him that the only people who came forward were his family and 2 close friends. Alisha's words never stopped ringing in his ears – *Be a man of substance, Aarav, not a man of substance abuse.* There was no access to any form of entertainment. Did those hostel guys and girls even know what he was going through? Did they care? He didn't think so, and that was a moment of awareness that dawned on his senses. No one else seemed to have input on how to detangle him from this situation. The power to change was in his hands, and that made him feel helpless and empowered, all at once. He was filled with a rather strange mix of gratitude and anger.

He remembered the fight he had with Dev on his wedding day. It was different since then, heavily awkward too because of how they both seemed to be invested in Alisha and they had to share the same house. Thank God they were looking at having a new home now, some privacy to look forward to, he thought, if he managed to get out of this facility soon enough.

'Hey….'

'Hey.'

He was curt, nothing new.

'Just wanted to check in on you.'

'Thanks, I'm fine.'

'Ok, take care. Call me if you need anything.'

Dev started to walk away. He felt so messed up. Part of him felt responsible for all this, but he was not, he told himself. This started long back. *Maybe Aarav was insecure of their friendship and hence?* Weird thoughts messed with his mind even more.

'Dev, wait.'

He turned around, surprised.

'Yeah, tell me?'

'Do you... did you... look at her like that? Did you love her?'

'No way. We have been friends since kindergarten, and you know how close we were. That's it. The fight we had on your wedding day was just a reaction to circumstances. What happened? Why are you asking me like that, all of a sudden?'

Dev shivered from within; he couldn't feel his insides. He felt he might faint. Did he know anything? Did he know about his feelings for her? There was no way. He hadn't even told Alisha, at that point.

'No, just, I'm sorry I said all that to you on my wedding day.'

'I'm sorry too. It wasn't becoming of me. I was worried for the both of you.'

'You never think of yourself, always for others.'

'No, it's not like that.'

'I understand that I put you in a dilemma. I shouldn't have done that...'

'Just take care of what you have; it is precious. Not everyone gets a chance, let alone a second one.'

'Thanks for having my back and helping me get on track. I appreciate it.'

'Always.'

With that, Dev walked out the door. A medley of emotions went through him. This was a big breakthrough; it had been years and years since they tried to get through to Aarav. They explained, pleaded, yelled. None of it worked. This was a last resort, and in actuality, no one had any hope. It was just something to try, to satisfy themselves that as family members, everyone did their bit. They tried a lot to convince him not to go haywire and to get help.

Wasn't this also an issue of the mind? Why would he not understand her anxiety when he himself was going through something extreme? It was unfair to all 3 of them; they were trapped in a web of chaos for years. Maybe this was the beginning of the end. Tears streaming down his face, he headed straight to the monastery. He didn't get out of the car for an hour. Then he finally got down and went to the meditation hall. He wanted to confess it all to someone, but he couldn't. He swore to himself to back off from their lives once Aarav got better.

She would not need him after that.

Chapter 9

Wait a little, breathe some more,
Let yourself watch 'you' grow.

'Stop using past references,' Dr Amar suggested.

'Meaning?' Alisha asked.

'It is a coping technique. When 2 people have reached a saturation point in their relationship and it seems like nothing will work out, whatever it is that you are trying to explain to each other, the past comes back, haunting and daunting. So, in severe cases, the only way to recoup is to stop using the past as a *reference* or *guideline*.'

He continued.

'The balance between 2 people is always swaying in any relationship. The key to maintaining a healthy balance is if both individuals have an equal voice to express themselves, to feel validated.

'When years pass and so much toxicity has already entered, it is close to impossible to peel the layers. But there are many ways to try and move on. One of the most effective ones is, whenever a new problem or a new argument/issue comes to face, do not use the past anger to rectify the present problem. That leads to unnecessary digging of things which happened, that brought out the worst in you or the opposite person; hence, past trauma returns to make healing all the more difficult.'

'But, doctor, if I don't bring up a past incident, how will the opposite person understand what I'm referring to? If it is something that is happening because of the same repetitive behaviour pattern, then only by magnifying the past will the person be able to understand the impact it is having on their present, isn't it?' Alisha was not able to agree with Dr Amar and was trying to debate what approach to use to further communicate with Aarav.

'No. If it had not reached saturation point, you could definitely use the past as a yardstick, a compass to navigate your relationship. *A past reference can be used as a good reference if the opposite person is willing to absorb the stability and solution the situation at hand is presenting.* But in this case, as is common to many relationships, you'll have revisited the past umpteen number of times already. After revisiting it constantly and seeing no benefit, the brain gets wired into only using it as a *defence mechanism* to avoid the topic, and it subconsciously feeds the same behaviour in both the people involved. It is like thrusting a ball into the water and trying your best to keep it there, but it will bounce back aggressively when you release it. Now you have to leave the ball to float and find its own course. Old wounds need time to heal, and a new set of behaviours and boundaries will do wonders for that. Without constantly being reminded, the necessary memories will surface by themselves. It is like a mental sedimentation with 3 steps –

- Acknowledging, experiencing, and forgiving one's thought process.
- Like sedimentation, letting one's thoughts settle down, undisturbed.
- Listening to the guiding voices behind the loud noises.'

Alisha was finding it hard to comprehend it all at the same time, but she knew it would make sense to her once she sat down to reflect on it. *Making changes in our own behaviour to initiate changes in the behaviour of the opposite person*, this is what she broadly understood.

'Now, coming to you, it's commendable that you have been off medication and have contained your emotions in a composed way, but it is not that if you feel helpless, you should never take medicine. Medicines are here to help us if we use them correctly, and there is no harm in that. There are a few approved SSRIs (Selective Serotonin reuptake inhibitors) which are safe for you now, but I would suggest it only on an SOS basis.'

'Can you tell me more about these reuptake inhibitors?'

'The brain has different chemicals... some of the prominent ones being serotonin, oxytocin, dopamine, and endorphins. Each plays a different role in balancing various moods and functions of the brain. Out of all these, serotonin is a mood stabiliser, so the reuptake inhibitors help the blood not absorb all of it, allowing the body to still use it when the person is experiencing depression, anxiety, and the like. This is what I meant when I explained to you that it is a normal experience, many people go through it.

'Anyway, coming back to the present situation, rehabilitation is a process. So try to give it some time, even if there is no progress. It means, in most cases, it is slow progress. And that is great. As long as there is no deterioration.'

'Thank you, doctor, for your time and advice, as always...' She got up carefully.

As she walked out of his cabin, memories flooded her. She remembered the days she used to dread the visits, and then she looked forward to them when the structured medication started doing their work. She remembered all those dreadful panic attacks, all the irrational thoughts, and dizziness. She never found too many people who would understand her, *but when she got help from the doctor, she felt hope, and that was magical, to see and experience a world outside her beliefs.* **Like a colour blind man seeing the rainbow for the first time.**

She started trying to explain to her friends and family the *importance of getting help and normalising certain feelings.* Not everyone understood, but the few who did were proud of Alisha. In time, so many people opened up. They were confident to express themselves because of her support. Yes, it would take a long time to make an entire community aware, but it's never too late to start, and if she couldn't make a difference to a billion people, she could try making a difference to at least one person. There is so much purpose and fulfilment in that.

With all the hard work she had done on herself, she had spoken to her doctor about creating a support group of sorts, but she didn't know how to go about it. He had given her a list of NGOs, organisations, and communities which would help her achieve something in her capacity. She also thought it would be a great idea to approach schools and colleges with curated seminars on Mental Health Awareness in an interactive way. She walked towards the exit with jitters and gratitude for being able to see the light at the end of that deep, dark tunnel she was in years ago, days after the first competition.

It was only her parents who knew about that dreadful night, not even Dev.

'What are you doing?' her mum asked.

'Nothing just…,' she seemed stiff and stoic.

'Come for dinner, dad is waiting.'

'Gimme a bit.'

After waiting for 15 minutes, she went back, and the room door was locked. Worriedly, she knocked loudly on the door. Nothing. Agitatedly, she started thumping the door. Alisha opened it a few minutes later, and it was obvious that she was completely distraught.

'What's wrong?' she shook her by the shoulders frantically. 'Arun,' she shrieked. He ran into the room but couldn't understand what was happening. He looked at Alisha and noticed her slurring and sweating, swaying. He helplessly looked around and noticed tablet covers all over the floor. 'What on Earth?' As he was trying to put 2 and 2 together, he realised that she had consumed all of them. An array of medication, some of hers, some of his, and some of her mum's,

nothing was making sense, and he couldn't understand why on Earth she had resorted to something so dangerous. He had immediately dialled an ambulance and rushed her to the hospital.

'She needs a stomach wash immediately,' the duty doctor had said.

They were so nervous and guilty. They should have paid heed at the right time.

It was an hour later when they could take a peaceful breath. 'She is fine, but luckily, you got her here in time,' he said.

After that incident, she understood that if she wanted to live any semblance of a normal life, she would have to step up and deal with her emotions head-on. She needed a structured medication plan, honest communication with her medics, and a break from all relationships which triggered or saturated her.

And she was grateful to have come out of it.

Chapter 10

The pains were a lot this time. It was different from the first time around. Alisha had been in labour for more than 4 hours. She was sweating and feeling cold in turns. How long was this wait?

Sara was restless and was sent home. Then, she got restless and came back to the hospital. She was insecure, probably. She wasn't cooperating or agreeing to spend time with anyone else. Alisha had spoken to her at length about this, and little Sara was more than excited to welcome a sibling. Children have different ways of expressing themselves, and at that moment, all she wanted was to be with her mother.

It was also the day of Aarav's discharge. An end to a six-month programme. *I want to be back home when the baby comes…* he had pleaded to Dev.

What a gruelling 6 months it had been. When he looked back, he trembled at the image of what he was just those few months ago. A few weeks prior to entering the facility, he found out that they were expecting again. He was overjoyed and paranoid at the same time. How would he fix the damage?

'It's just for 6 months,' Alisha coaxed him. 'We need to start over, if you want to, that is!'

'Just for 6 months? It's not a few days or weeks, Alisha. It is 6 whole months! Do you even realise how tough it is going to be on me? I am fine, you guys are just being dramatic. I don't need this ridiculous programme to make me feel better,' he retorted.

'Absolutely nothing about this is fine. When you can begin to tell night from day and right from wrong, then you can say you're fine,' she snapped back.

She was exhausted with the constant quarrelling and was looking all over the city for a facility. When nothing seemed to make sense in terms of finance, logistics, and convenience, Dev (as usual) stepped in and comforted her. He took 2 months to propose and authorise this programme from the committees on board, and only after that, they could begin.

The first 2 months were utter chaos for Aarav. He would be restless throughout the night and sleepy during the day. He would blatantly avoid questions from doctors and not cooperate on any level with the faculty. He wasted food and time. His mother spent hours outside the waiting room, sometimes for days at a stretch, but he would only acknowledge her with irritation.

The peace and quiet time gave him so much distress initially; he did not know what to do with himself. He would constantly ring the call bell from his room, and when the attendant came in, he would ask for silly things like, *can I go outside for a walk, just one cigarette please,* and so on. He gave the counsellors the hardest time by refusing to speak, no matter how much they tried. *This is so stupid,* he thought to himself.

'I think it is best we don't try this hard,' Dr Pranav, the senior doctor in charge of the faculty, was telling them 2 weeks into the programme.

'What does that mean, doctor?' Alisha was flustered, completely at her wits end. 'If we don't try, then what is the purpose of this?'

'His case is different, Alisha. He is an extremely stubborn man. He has a way with his words, and he is not allowing a breakthrough of any sort for me or my team to get in. I cannot put him on medication because we are emphasising on a detox programme, and luckily he doesn't need it yet. But the more we try to ask him questions, the more he is going into a shell. He is yet very angry, so my suggestion would be to pause the therapy sessions until he himself wants to talk. It is like the old adage goes – we can take the horse to the water, but can't make him drink it. So let us not try to dig in too much, in the hope that he will himself take a step forward and be willing to talk to us.'

She was upset. How is he going to make a recovery when he doesn't even feel that this addiction is a problem? He was a hard nut to crack. She knew she could not extend this for more than 6 months. At that point, he would never agree, and it was also tough on their pockets.

'He needs to *feel* that something is wrong, to be able to heal from it,' Dev intervened.

They decided to just do their regular check-ins for the next 2 weeks and check if he was getting curious or interested in the change of arrangement.

It was only after the second month of being there that reality started sinking into his mind. He sat with himself, with his truth, with his agony. He felt a sense of shame. Having been as enterprising as a youth, he was a rather worn-down adult. He didn't know himself without his addictions. But he was presented with a choice in that moment and didn't know which path to take. People have it hard enough when circumstances force them to take a path; he was stupid to put himself in this delusion. The days that followed gave him a lot of silent space in his mind. He hardly had any interaction with anyone, and the little human interaction he had was with the fellow patients. There were very few people at that moment since the programme was a completely new one, the first one to be curated and conducted. There were just 5 other people apart from Aarav, and there was one man among them who was also there battling anxiety. He learnt so much about the ailment from him. His awareness increased multifariously regarding the subject and its various shades about how it can affect a person. It was then that his conversation with Dev helped him recognise himself.

Chapter 11

Naina was waiting at the reception, wondering what was taking Dev so long. He finally came in 15 minutes later.

'What took you so long?'

'Sorry! HOD duties now!'

'Aaron is waiting to meet you,' she blushed.

Naina was ecstatic and newly in love. She had met Aaron at a conference in New Delhi. She travelled often and never paid attention to making friends or socialising, or anything apart from her work, but Aaron had challenged her findings, and they got talking on the pretext of disagreeing with their respective approaches to their theses. It was intriguing and intellectual, and the more time they spent, the more they developed a beautiful understanding. They were poles apart, and that called for the perfect attraction.

'Love finds you when you least expect it,' Dev teased. He had never seen her blush. She looked pretty, made an effort to line her eyes and neaten her hair. She was suddenly dainty and demure, and love really does change people while making sure they stay exactly the same. It was quite amusing.'

'How are things? How long more does Aarav need to be here?' she enquired.

'A couple of months, that's it. Yeah, he is a lot better. Unless he is pretending, but I don't think so, I hope not.' *That'll be another level of madness*, he thought to himself. They made a couple of breakthroughs. But what is surprising is that, in most cases, we have seen these kinds of issues relate to deep repressed emotions, hidden trauma, and crazy emotional baggage. You know, a heavy load of information for the team to work on. With Aarav, it is so blank. There is nothing. It's just sad that from having a great life he just got into stupid company and it has influenced him to this extent.' They chatted as they were walking towards the new restaurant down the road.

'Yeah, I mean. It is weird. But in any case, all's well that ends well, right? How is Al?'

He stiffened, but she didn't notice. She was replying to a message on the phone.

'Yeah, she's fine,' he kept it abrupt.

'And how are you?' she looked sharply into his eyes, those eyes that couldn't lie to her.

'I don't know, how does it matter anyway?'

'What do you mean, how does it matter? Of course, it matters.'

'I don't think about it. There is a lot going on all the time.'

'Are you in touch with Isha?'

'No, that ended long ago. She got bored listening to my stories about Alisha! Haha!'

She could sense the pain in his voice. *What a resilient man he was,* she thought.

He was charmed by Aaron and happy for his friend. They ate a delightful meal before heading home. Naina called him after their dinner.

'So, what do you think?'

'He seems like a great guy! I'm so happy for you!'

'He is, isn't he?' She couldn't hide her happiness.

'Listen,' she continued. 'I'm worried, you've gone so quiet. I get that a lot is happening, but suddenly you seem different. Has anything gone wrong with Al and you?'

Dev shook from within. Why was he constantly being asked about this, by her, his parents, even Aarav asked him if they met recently?

'No, nothing. What was going right, anyway, for it to go wrong?' he joked.

'Look, Naina. I've just been trying to piece them back together. Sara is young, and they just need to find themselves back. I need to be there through it, and then I'm off.'

'Off to where? Please don't say the monastery now!'

'Nah! I don't know. I don't want to think about it. But I can't be this involved anymore. It's taking a toll on me.'

She stayed silent, not knowing what to say. She worried for her friend.

'I will call you soon, take care.'

Dev turned off his bedside light and turned it back on a million times before he fell asleep that night.

Chapter 12

'The registrations will close this week, Alisha.'

Anthony Sir spoke in a slow voice. He was older now; he wasn't conducting classes. Alisha was one of the main students and faculty of the prestigious institution.

'I will try to sing tomorrow, Sir.'

'Try, if not, we will look into it next time.'

Her heart sank. She wanted this so bad. But what sense did it make when she knew she couldn't give it her one hundred percent? She knew he was so eager to see her perform on a national podium as well, but it would have to wait.

'Why do you have to pressurise yourself again?' her mother reprimanded. 'You have achieved so much. Now is the time to take care of yourself and the children. Then, when you get stronger, you can always get back to it. No need to be so emotional now.'

'Mama, I don't want to be lectured right now, please.' She could barely eat her dinner.

'You need it. You will constantly be thinking about this, and you will drive yourself crazy. You need to understand everything has its timing. If you rush to participate now, you will not be able to give it your all. And besides, you will get a million opportunities. This is just my suggestion; the rest is up to you.'

After a lot of thought and deliberation, she decided that there was no point in participating at that moment. She paid attention to what her mum told her; everything would have its timing. No need to rush things.

She was in the peak of her time, but she knew if she went ahead with something half-heartedly, the outcome would be the same. It was too risky to sing at that point. She could barely speak a few sentences without getting breathless. She was unsure if she would recover as soon as the competition needed her.

She recalled the time when her parents got to know of Aarav's habits. They felt so terribly bad for their daughter and so upset at his deceitfulness, they could barely believe this is what had been going on.

'Come back,' her dad had told her. And that really shattered her confidence. She thought he would tell her to fight things through; people are not supposed to give up on one another, that was what he had always taught her. Nothing is meant to be if we don't work towards it; they brought her up with those strong sense of values. To watch her entire sense of self being questioned, her parents questioning their set of beliefs, was the toughest phase of all. That was the point she lost all her faith in her marriage.

It was a few days later when she told her parents that she wanted to work on her marriage and not come back. Marrying Aarav was a choice she made, and however free a thinker she had tried to be, a part of her knew it would not be fair to leave without trying every possible solution to get this fixed. Still, if it didn't work, then that would be a different story.

She snapped back to the present. Since she had all the time in the world now, she was surprised to find herself so relieved. She could focus on Aarav's recovery and spend quality time with Sara. With the little one coming, they had much to prepare for.

She took on a full-time responsibility at the studio. She was in charge of everything, heading administration, recruitments, and training. She wanted to be as involved and continued in that role post her delivery as well. Anthony Sir was more than happy to have her on board full time. It was her safe space, after all.

Chapter 13

'I think she should be ready to deliver anytime now,' the doctor told her parents.

'But doctor, you said it would be around 10 am... the father will only be here around 9...' Arun replied worriedly. It was a promise they had made to each other, to be together to welcome the little one.

'Just a few minutes, Saru,' Arun was cradling his granddaughter on his lap. The poor girl was so tired but wouldn't fall asleep.

It was 4 am in the morning.

'Where is papa?' she kept asking.

Asha was inside the room, taking care of Alisha through the pains.

Arun decided to call Dev. He wanted Aarav to be there, somehow.

'Yes Sir, but it seems it may be a lot sooner... we will prepare anytime now...' He got busy with the rest of his team.

Dev rubbed his eyes...*Has she delivered already?* was his first thought. He had been staying on the premises the entire week. He had made a promise to Aarav to take him home with his family. He had to keep up his word.

'Yes, uncle?'

'Bring him, son.'

The sun was still hiding in the night sky when Dev went into the dorm room to awaken Aarav, who was restless in his sleep, too. He couldn't wait for this day to come, to return home, a new man, a new mind, and a new life.

'Is it time?'

'Yes, I've signed the documents. Let's go. Your discharge summary is with me. Your follow-up is next week. I have taken care of the formalities last week itself.'

'Thank you, Dev,' Aarav came forward and hugged his younger brother tight.

Through the tiny window lattice, he saw the first rays of the sun shining into the dim room.

They drove out of the campus and straight to the hospital.

Their parents would arrive at any time, too.

As soon as they arrived, Aarav rushed into the labour ward. They handed him a mask and scrubs, and he went inside. It felt like time had paused. He remembered being there for Sara too, and now, after what felt like a dream or a nightmare, he couldn't make up his mind....there he was, back again, ready to be reunited with his family.

Alisha could barely believe her eyes when she saw him standing there. Relief and happiness took over her. They had met just the previous week, and he showed the promise of a new life to her. He told her he would be there, and here he was, ready to be the pillar she needed.

Dev caught a glimpse of Alisha through the ruffling curtains and stepped back. *Not my place to be here anymore,* he thought to himself.

It was just about 17 minutes later when he was born. Elation filled the room; tears of joy and happiness filled their hearts, and little Saru was over the moon. Nicky was finally here!

Chapter 14

Never give up on your hardest fight,
Your darkness shines someone else's light.

'Here, take some more…' Aarav served her some of the freshly brewed chamomile tea he made. It was weird for her. He was so different. They were trying to make sense of each other in a brand new way.

They sat together in front of the television to watch a movie, probably for the second time in their married life. He went closer to her; he didn't want her to wince. The kids were fast asleep, but she knew Nikhil would wake up in 3 hours; he had settled into a routine. Nikhil was just a few months old, and she had her hands full. The days would pass in the studio, and she had resumed training. Her voice was back to being strong, and she practiced religiously 5 days a week.

They had some time to themselves now. It felt scary. *Trying to build a new dynamic in an old relationship isn't that simple.* The new apartment they had moved to was a blessing, away from their past; at least, it was easier to convince themselves. It was time to start over, they felt.

He had settled into a job. It was a boring 9-5 routine, but that boredom was the best thing that happened to him. He appreciated the monotony as it gave him a sense of stability, structure, and discipline when he was around her. And then, he found new ways to get intoxicated, *ways that she would never know of.*

She had so much to be grateful for. Getting him back from the dark depths of his mind was something she would always be immensely thankful for. Not everyone gets another chance. But in the midst of it all, she often wondered if they would be able to share something real. She had only known an addicted version of him. That changed a lot of things in her mind.

Her children were fortunately younger at the time, and only a small percentage of people improve so dramatically and get to erase parts of their past. Not everyone was blessed with so many opportunities and forgiving families. Sara and Nikhil were fortunate; they didn't get to absorb their parents' toughest days, and that was the biggest blessing for them as parents. To be able to provide for their children was a privilege indeed… It was mostly thanks to Dev's efforts, she often thought to herself.

He had been the rock-solid person through it all with her, insisted on a detox with in-depth counselling, curated a recuperation programme (which went on to become a statutory part of the services the institution had to offer), had stuck by her, and tried to protect her every step of the way, and tried to find out what had caused Aarav to shift from being a starry-eyed youth to a blindsided addict. He was there through it all, even when there was *nothing* in it for him to gain.

Those piercing pangs of pain would never leave Alisha. She knew that in an alternate reality, she would have lived being her best self and not left him in the lurch. Not him, not for every single thing he had continuously done for her.

As for Dev, he never really did move on. He lived in the shadow of a love he had lost but saw almost every other day. He convinced himself that he was happy to be a part of the same people, the same family, and the starkly different reality.

He went to the faded blue bench every other day, to remind himself of the greatest love he knew.

Epilogue

The air brimmed with magic. The light drizzle added to the dreamy atmosphere. It felt like déjà vu. The same feeling ran through her, as if the clock had rewound twenty-five long years. The journey, oh! The journey, the failures, the stepping stones, the challenges. And yet, here she stood, after being crowned the winner at *India's Nightingale*. What a moment, what an honour, and what a blessed opportunity to have had the chance to participate and win.

Alisha was invited as the chief guest at the Republic Day Parade. *This moment was bigger than winning the competition.* It was her dream many, many years ago; she remembered Mrs. Devon fondly in her crisp lemon-coloured silk sari. She had envisioned herself at the dais singing the anthem of our country, a moment of pride, a moment that would be etched in the history of Ridge Maidan. She stood proudly, dressed in a light shade of a pink damask print sari. Age had changed so much of her appearance, but not her demeanour.

Aarav, Sara, and Nikhil were seated in the front with Alisha to watch the parade. Being the family of the chief guest, they had access to being seated right in the front. They watched the procession in awe. The thrill in the air was inexplicable.

'Please welcome our Chief Guest, Mrs. Alisha...' Her name was announced to go up on stage and do the honour of hoisting the flag. As they introduced her and spoke about her contribution in the field of Arts & Music, she received accolades for her various performances. Pictures were taken for the press and media, and she was called to come up in front on the dais, where the mic was placed for her to sing.

Alisha rose and walked up to the front. A few words later, she requested everyone to stand to attention as they began the solemn ceremony of the flag hoisting. With a heart bursting in pride and a voice trembling with emotion, she gracefully sang the anthem.

At the end of what was a lovely evening, the 4 of them sat down in their living room, waiting for their respective families and friends to join in any moment....

The dining table was set with a scrumptious buffet, and everyone was waiting to celebrate the momentous occasion...

Soon, the house was filled with people. Alisha's parents chatted away with Aarav, and the grandchildren, distant cousins, and common friends were catching up after a long time. Colleagues and friends from the studio had come too.

Dev was there too. He had missed the ceremony, but he was sure he would watch the recording in his alone time. *He would not want to miss out on watching the moment, the moment his best friend had worked towards for years together... of Alisha living her biggest dream.*

'Congratulations, mama!' Sara had prepared a cute cake for her mum to cut. They had always been so close, and she was thrilled and proud of her mum! She knew how much this moment meant to her!

'Come, come closer, dad! Uncle Dev, come join in!'

'Where is Nikhil?' Aarav was looking around the house.

'Must be doodling, drawing, or writing, what else?' Sara grinned. 'He is so much like you, Dev uncle! Not only in the way that he looks, but even in his habits and interests!'

Dev parted his lips in a sombre smile. He had been so quiet for the last few years.

Alisha looked away before they could make any eye contact.

Aarav made sure he was sober on that day. He didn't want to give anyone an inkling of his habits after the rehabilitation programme. As luck would have it, Akshay contacted him years ago; it seemed like inducing drugs in the form of needles was the new thing. Alisha could never see the incoherence in his eyes, or his walk, and that was enough for him to silently continue whenever and wherever he found an opportunity.

Once Aarav got back from the rehabilitation programme a few years ago, Dev & Alisha didn't speak as much as they used to. It was too difficult to balance both the relationships, and this worked better, with her being able to give her family her time and presence. She was so busy with her vocal training that she rarely got time away from her responsibilities. She had participated in India's Nightingale for the fourth time when she was crowned the winner. She didn't mind not making it; she just loved having a reason to keep training and aiming for it.

'Congratulations, Alisha.' Dev spoke softly. They were standing close to each other, but they had never been further apart from each other.

They tried a lot not to think about it that night, but neither of them was able to erase their memories. Somewhere in the ocean of their thoughts, there was one wave that kept coming back to remind them of their weakness.

It was years since that incident had taken place. In the ever-changing constant of their lives, they were punished to be around each other forever, to live a big lie around the million smaller truths… never having an opportunity to talk things through or even share the same space anymore. What use would it be to discuss it? The only relief was that it was over. The decision taken by them to get a separate apartment was the wisest thing to do. What choice did they have?

It was the night before he came back from Delhi, and a few days before he finally went to the rehabilitation centre.

That one night, many years ago, Alisha had gone down for a walk.

Things had just started getting volatile with Aarav, and the only form of intimacy they shared was physical, which saturated her, but she didn't know how to break free. They had stopped communicating; he couldn't understand her.

She wanted to leave, but where would she go? Dr Amar had suggested trying a rehabilitation centre, but he would never agree. He would lash out in anger because he was always drunk and then apologise in the morning when he was sober. She was sick of everything, especially the vicious circle they seemed to be stuck in.

After a few weeks, Aarav was in Delhi for some work conference (or so he claimed), and Sara was spending the weekend at her grandparents. In the twilight, she had bumped into Naina. They got chatty and went to get a bite somewhere close by. Alisha decided on a glass of wine for the first time. 'What is all this talk about? High time I tried it too.' She giggled with Naina, trying to mask her agitations.

It was a fun evening, she remembered. But Naina said things she should not have. She had told Alisha about the old days. Days of Dev's struggle, his desire to be with her, his regret about not saying anything when he had the chance.

She asked her how she took it when he confessed his feelings to her. He had confessed his feelings? What was she talking about? It had been a long time. Naina didn't know she was going to open old wounds.

'He came to meet you when your voice didn't respond in that first competition. Aarav asked him if he could speak to you first… he saw you 2 together….' She felt the room spinning around her. Was she hearing things right?

Alisha was preoccupied for the rest of the dinner. She tried to stay calm but couldn't. She rushed through her meal, and after they were done, she frantically rushed to

Dev's house. It was drizzling, but she continued to walk. He had taken an apartment close by after his degree, which he used only for his study and research purposes. She had been there only once, with the family. Luckily, he opened the door, and she stood there, transparent and drenched in the rain.

'Hi! Come in. Is everything okay?' he asked, genuinely concerned.

'Dev, I'm sorry to have come unannounced at this hour. I bumped into Naina today. I get that we haven't spoken about this in a long time. Things changed, and we both know how and why, but losing you was the worst feeling in my life. Today, she asked me how I took it when you confessed your feelings to me. I knew you said it hurt you, but I never knew you felt this way about me. How, how could you not tell me anything, Dev? And then she told me about all those years of your struggle, of your desire to leave everything behind because it didn't work between us…I knew you were hurt, but I didn't know you loved me that much.'

'How… how could you have never said anything to me? All those years?'

Alisha burst into tears. She could not stop talking; it was like opening up Pandora's Box. She was on medication again, but right now her anxiety had hit the roof. She started trembling, and Dev finally broke. He went to her, put his arms around her, and cried. They were not able to separate from each other; they sank into the sofa in his very small living room. 'Help me out,' she had whispered. 'I will, I will think of something and get it done…' They held on to each other for a long, long silent time. 'Are we being punished? Why didn't you stop me from anything?'

Nothing about this moment was right; she was married to his brother. It was against every value they had. But they were locked in a deep embrace for a long time. He had to hold her now. He told her that when he had rushed to tell her the night her voice didn't respond, he knew she needed him then, how she was hurting – when she lost the Voice of Himachal contest. But Aarav had requested him to let him talk to her first. That night was the night he wanted to tell her everything. Before she and Aarav could even start, she and Dev had already ended.

He spoke about how eager he was to tell her at that moment itself, better late than never. Aarav would understand in time, but when he saw them both kissing in the rain, it felt like the finish line. He told her how dejected he was through it all, how he forced himself to put on a brave face because he really didn't know how to express himself. His years of regret, which was still why he could not move on, could not be in a relationship with anybody. The fight they had on their wedding day. His constant visits to the monastery to just feel disconnected from his reality. He didn't want to have a family if it was not with her.

Alisha could not control herself. It took her years to realise that it was a kind of love she never knew could take form. She never looked at herself as separate from him. But Aarav and she were married now, albeit unhappily, but what could she do? She did not want to leave him; she loved him too. Surely, she had to be by his side in his darkness and bring him back to the light.

The guilt was beginning to rise in both of them. In that terrible moment of weakness, they had their moment of strength. That one night, they had lived the love of a million lifetimes. They were completely immersed in each other, absorbed in every part of the other. They couldn't stop themselves from feeling those feathers of emotion that had been swirling around them their whole lives. It was their moment, where every single thing they knew and believed in, completely refused to exist. It was indeed the essence of self-expression and the epitome of self-destruction. It was a night they would never be able to forgive themselves for, and it was the night that gave closure to their love story.

The only thing she kept from that night was a small piece of paper, in which he had written a small heartfelt poem, with big feelings. He had named it 'The Dance'. He didn't intend to give it to her; she had found it on his study and asked him questions about it. They had read it together, and she had kept it in her bag later, her wet fingers creating blotches of ink all over the paper... after all these years, the writing had faded away... just like every other thing does...

Trapped in morality, freed in reality.

They never spoke about that to each other after that day, living the pretence that it never even happened.

And no one would have to know about this bitter truth, not Aarav, not Dev, not Nikhil.

The Dance

Rain, from azure skies...

Glows an early moon through branches,

That fall and rise...

(The deeper they fall, the higher they rise.)

Mirror the light in a whirlpool of convenience...

A will tampered by resistance.

This is the stage, the arena of all sentience.

Conferred with supremacy, to engender what I wish will be…

(I am anonymous to me)

Aren't we all granted with the same powers?

We all are…

And then we dance to everyone's tunes,

But ours.

For what is ours but hope of being a part of what contains parts of our soul?

Aren't we all parts of that same divine force?

Which split us and unite us and recreated the same dance in which we are manoeuvred, in many ways.

In accordance with the conflict,

Of the avaricious mind that wants thee,

And the pleading heart, to set your soul free.

My hands rise up to the tune.

My feet glide through the ground.

My ears can hear the sound of the universe shattering in this quiet body... dancing the dance of all life... the dance of all beyond life...

My eyes see night and day, see sun and snow.

See war and peace

See creation from destruction.

All in a transient sparkle illuminating each soul, near and far.

For none do differ, all collide at par.

I see everything in nothing.

Icy, imprecise movement... I slowly gyrate

To this dance, fusing the variance of fate.

You... stand behind me, hold me,

Till my heart beats with yours.

Till I can hear you breathe.

Dancers of the cosmic dance.

(Fly away, yes... once the dance is over.)

Our souls are but dancers, not the dance.

And if there might be a path, ushering us to the end,

Let it come to vision, all of we are yet to comprehend,

Dance with me, till I can set you free.

Partner in rhyme,

Under the divine light, we shine.

For but one moment in time,

Eternal.